VELVET
NIGHTMARES

CHINA HAMILTON

VELVET NIGHTMARES
ER BOOKS
London 2009

ER Books
Email: enquiries@eroticprints.org
Web: www.eroticprints.org

ER Books is a publisher of fine art, photography and fiction books and limited editions. To find out more please visit us on the web at
www.eroticprints.org

ISBN 978-1-904989-59-2

CHINA HAMILTON

VELVET
NIGHTMARES

INDEX

Uncharted lands, lost territories
Ancient dark myths and children's ghost stories
Hanging from hooks and hanging on words,
Kisses on foreheads and screaming of birds.
And all of the little ones, lost and alone
Cry for their supper and beg to go home.

I MAGINATION. THE SEAT OF CREATIVITY AND INSPIRATION, THE home of entire worlds of possibility. For an artist, imagination is one of the first requirements our commitment to our art demands. Yet we can wake up one day, with our lives half over, to discover the lies we were programmed with so young would love to ride us to our graves. As a daughter of the California women's movement, I was taught that thoughts are things. That what we think, our fantasies, and our minds, must be censored and controlled, or we risk betraying our sisters and ourselves. I woke up to this lie, in anger and frustration, at the age of 48 and realised that if I couldn't be absolutely honest with myself, how could I ever be so with anyone else? How would I ever become the artist I knew I was capable of being? The time had come to release those forbidden thoughts and see where they would lead me.

As luck would have it, the first place I found was ChinaHamilton. com, a deliciously edgy world created by a very dark mind. This was quickly followed by a gift of his book, *Bittersweet Sex*, still the best illustration I have ever found of my childhood fantasies. Someone else saw what I saw. I had found a like-minded traveller. Our friendship over the ensuing years has largely been based on an exchange of thoughts and ideas, emails and phone calls. The China Hamilton that I know is an inspiring artist. His medium changes often, and includes photography, video, and paint, as well as the written word. I have been privileged to witness and share some of his expeditions into the darkness ahead. I have a particular soft spot for what I call his disturbing little vignettes, and have always hoped one day they would be embraced within a little collection that would fit into my pocket.

China Hamilton's stories are not for the faint-hearted, nor should they be confused with reality. Like his photographs, I find them challenging and courageous. Even in the realms of BDSM, some may find a few of these tales uncomfortable places to visit. It depends on what you are looking for. Do you want a nice bit of essential bedtime reading? Or do you want to venture into uncharted waters? The latter is probably a more appropriate description in this case. Is it erotica? Is it even sex? In truth, I don't know. What I *do* know however, is that it pries open my mind, races my blood and lets the demons out to play.

And god I love those demons...

Constance Redgrave
December 2008

I T IS NEVER EASY TO INTRODUCE SUCH AN ECLECTIC SELECTION of sometimes dark, often cruelly sadistic and certainly intentionally erotic short stories. Having said that, there are also here some softer and more gentle tales as the simple pursuit of sexual pleasure will never fail to please in fiction. I have been writing such things for many years occasionally published under other names and this work has run along side my photographic art. I do not see these activities as separated but rather unified sides of my work in this creative field and products of my sexually adventurous mind.

It is all an expression of my all-consuming fascination with the erotic fantasies of women, especially those that explore my eternal muse, which I simplistically sum up as, '*power, pain and pleasure*'. *Power*, of course explores the complexities of domination, submission, humiliation and degradation. *Pain*, involves the use of such forces, emotional and physical, to apply the instruments of power that are the most human of perverse contemplations... "what would it really feel like to experience that, to become a victim, or even to be in the dominant role?" *Pleasure*, is the often private, secret reward that flows from all fantasies, real or imagined.

This confirms that women will be at the centre of my themes, sometimes as those in control, sometimes engaged upon adventures, quite often as willing or unwilling victims of dark, cruel, sexual forces. This does not, however, preclude the male from sharing and enjoying but the stimulation and source of most of my written work comes from the minds of women, who have, over the years, been so kind as to share with me their erotic thoughts and delights. I have been constantly surprised by the often extreme darkness, sadism and cruelty of their private fantasies. Even more surprised when apparently even the most conventional and respectable, even publicly prudish, amongst them sometimes share with me a detailed taste of the mysteries of what really lights their intimate fires.

There are a few writers of the erotic that have achieved the hallowed ground of 'great art'. I do not see my stories as such – my place is the role of journeyman, rather than creative master. The short story suits these themes as most sexual experiences live but for a few hours, some flashes of sexual thought even only a few seconds, so I tell the tales much in the way that they flow through my own mind or as they were recounted to me. I have never before seen them as a collection for a book but rather up to now as brief escapes as I pass moments of the day or drive in the car remembering and enjoying the accounts that have been shared with me. Then when down on paper to share them with some female friends.

I make no apologies for my 'heroines' sometimes suffering seemingly awful experiences. The contemplation by proxy of the most dreaded and feared is an eternal desire or else writers and filmmakers would have no audience. Neither would we so often delight in either taking part in dangerous pursuits or watching others take the risks. We seek many escapes and many roles and directions to achieve our adrenalin highs or erotic moments and the possession of a strong imagination is one of the unique gifts our development has given us. We must rejoice in it and welcome its private moments of pleasure and stimulation. Quite accurately, the past world was a cruel and sadistic place; as some stories turn back the clock, so will they reflect the harshness of those times.

I have been fascinated by the reactions and comments of my small 'test panel' of readers with whom I have shared, over the years, each story. They have all been female but each are different, some even, as I have said, deeply respectable! One thing they have in common is their desire to read more. An often repeated observation, usually applied to the most powerful and disturbing stories, is that they enjoyed the story and could erotically transpose themselves into the role of the victim, yet were at the same time shocked that they wanted to be there in their fantasy. They were and are confused by this dual reaction. Many have the susceptibility to be attracted to the complexity of the Stockholm Syndrome, seeking in their imagination that the strange and compelling blurring of roles and lines become intertwined emotionally, oppressed and oppressor.

The darker worlds of the human extreme, and its obvious sexual, sadistic and masochistic attraction to so many of us, intrigue me. My stories are based upon fact, moments in history and actual practice, others, as I have explained come from shared fantasies, some even from the actual, personal experiences of my friends. I have never needed to invent a method of punishment or torture for better minds than mine have been so cruelly creative in real life and history. What people have often experienced in their daily existence and recounted to me is also far more creative than any make believe I could contrive. Equally, many texts and accounts have come down to us and can be turned into a narrative. What must be remembered is that, in all cases, these are fantasies, that the real and so often cruel world is a different and serious place. Perhaps we like the fiction because it helps us to deal with the sadness of reality?

The greatest problem I always have to confront is pleasing every one, male or female with my writing. Of course an impossible task. Some quite valid areas of human sexuality have been avoided for they are beyond my own mind to enjoy or conjure. Some other areas are also avoided because they are plainly unacceptable to me, even as a fantasy. I have also attempted to steer clear of too much 'detail' for it can make writing seem more like a 'D.I.Y.' manual. However, sometimes detail is necessary to explain a procedure or clarify an experience successfully. I apologise if that D.I.Y. manual occasionally appears, for I know that it can be just as much fun for the reader's imagination to fill in the gaps.

I have tried to provide something for most tastes. It will be found that some 'themes' and 'attractions' are repetitive, like the varied attentions to the female bottom. In this I am an observer of the universality of human nature. This round form is after all a most beautiful thing and as with beauty we love it or love to desecrate it, or enjoy both tastes simultaneously. It is also true that with sexual fantasy it is the physical symbols of sexuality that most focus attention. Historically, especially when men have performed the punishments, they have focused upon the symbols of feminity.

Robert Held, writes in his extraordinary book "Inquisition"…
"And since the soul of torture is male and in the tenebrosity of his unilluminable nature the male is terrified by the mysteries of the female's cycles and fecundity but above all by her inherent intellectual, emotional and sexual superiority, these organs that define her essence have forever been subjected to his most savage ferocity, he being superior only in physical strength."

Flagellation, generally speaking, always draws an audience much as it did when public whipping posts graced every town. Female pubic hair will seem often to be removed, sadly I fear for those lovers of the wondrous bush, for today few sexually active women do more than sport some minimal artistic coiffure, if any. Equally the Middle East and beyond has always favoured depilation. When women were incarcerated it was also often trimmed short, as was the hair upon their heads: this action to prevent lice. Where punishment and torture played their dark roles it was again common to remove it so better to gain clear access to this most sensitive of places and, of course, to humiliate by exposure. It was, for example, removed when women were seen as witches and were to be 'pricked' and searched for the teats of their familiars and secreted magical objects. It was inevitably removed by the infamous Inquisition who almost always singed it away with a lighted wax taper as the first stage in a female's examination for the same reasons. The text of the Inquisition, the *Malleus Maleficarum* insists, as part of its guidance and instruction for interrogators, that women be stripped fully and shorn of all their bodily hair, least they hide any witch's devices within. Is it not far more likely that a misogynistic desire to humiliate lay behind their zeal?

I have also provided a few less scary and demanding stories that explore nothing more complicated than simple sex.

In the end, do not be embarrassed to enjoy, for our minds as yet remain uncensored and free. Try not to have wet nightmares.

China Hamilton

I THE BRASS BED

This is a 'sweet' and gentle story, a calm refuge from other places...

IT WAS JUST AFTER HER EIGHTEENTH BIRTHDAY that Fifine moved from her home, a flower-covered cottage amid a scurry of fields and knotted woodland to the south of the city of Antwerp. In her place of birth she had so happily grown up, sharing laughter and surprises with her friends, the love of her parents and the endeavours of the village school and its earnest, cleric master.

That life was now behind her. For it was with her aunt that she had come to live, in a house in the crumbling and neglected part of the city. The aunt, at the request of her parents, had found her a job working in the untidy, strangely-smelling office of a small factory that provided all kinds of paints and varnishes for the polishing trade.

Most girls of the age that Fifine had gained would have found the combination of the musty, drab old town house, the kind but exceptionally 'maiden' aunt, who lived surrounded by unfulfilled memories and finally the cramped office with its pungent smells, intolerable. Fifine however was different. She positively adored the ramble of streets and the urgency and energy of the new surroundings. Her aunt's house... "Oh, so many rooms, how large, how grand..." and her job. She was important. She had responsibility. She loved it all, this sheltered country girl.

To explore and expand her knowledge of her surroundings, she would take a different route home from work each day. She would walk these cobbles, head thrown back, her hair a tumble of exciting auburn curls. Her face would elicit smiles and nods from those she passed, for Fifine's pure complexion, honed by the clean air and fresh rains of her youth and bathed in her eager appreciation, would cheer these folk. Her progress was often slow for she was determined to examine every strange alley and to probe the corners of every shop window. So it was on such a walk home, venturing into new territory, that she was met by a sprawl of books that engulfed the pavement before her and acted as an advance guard for the shop that seemed to be full to the very brim with all shapes and sizes of tattered and discarded volumes.

As an only child she had so often filled her time by reading and escaping into the pictures of fantasy that the words created, so when confronted by such a cornucopia of books it was natural that she should actually dare to venture into the shop. The smell of old leather and damp paper hit her like a wall. The sprung bell over the door rang and clattered disturbingly, and for while she moved freely in amongst the enticing shelves that curved under their weight as no one came to attend to her.

At first, as the door had closed on its old spring and the noise of the street outside was subdued, she felt a little shy, an intruder in the musty silence that had descended. Plucking up courage she selected a leather bound book at random. It turned out to be a volume of poems. Her eyes, now accustomed to the dim light, sought out the first line of a verse. As she read on, she was suddenly aware of a presence beside her. Silently it seemed he had appeared, a man in his mid thirties of dark complexion. He was dressed in a faded black suit with a gold chain joining the two halves of his waistcoat. His face seemed to radiate some kind of understanding, even kindness, and as his eyes held hers she quickly recovered from the initial shock.

It was, at first, a moment when both were without words and the clock moved so slowly as it does at such times. It was Fifine who at last broke the spell being unable to hold his steady gaze. She demurely dropped her eyes back to the book and she heard him ask, in a most normal way, if she was just browsing or could he perhaps be of help with a special request for a specific book? Ordinary as the question was, it seemed to strangely overwhelm her and she found herself actually blushing without knowing why. He spoke again, words that now she didn't even hear, only shyly looking up just enough to see his lips move. Fifine was transfixed as he turned and drew a fine, slim volume from an adjacent shelf. He was smiling now, just a little, and his long, sensitive fingers parted the pages with deliberate delicacy, almost reverence, as one would carefully open the petals of a flower. He brought the volume to his mouth and Fifine looked on in wonder as he puckered his lips and blew a small cloud of dust from the pages of the book. Fifine was so held by the voice that she didn't truly register what was being said, as she was also frozen by watching his face and his expressive hands. He was now speaking about the book, describing, excited and she nodded and murmured as a token of understanding in an attempt not to seem rude.

Feelings that Fifine had never before experienced surged through her body. They were unfamiliar but warm, disturbing but not unwelcome. The man returned the book and withdrew another. Again, the hands performed the little ritual of opening. As she watched this, new tensions gripped Fifine and contracted the muscles of her hard stomach before moving down to that place between her thighs of which she was only dimly aware. She had been conscious for many years of little tremors in that place of which no one talked and her mother had treated the onset of her first menstruation with some ill-disguised horror. Now the feeling there grew to a level she had never experienced and she wanted to squirm and to touch it to such an extent that she started to shift her weight from foot to foot as though she needed to pee. She parted her legs in an attempt to let the building pressure escape, but instead this produced a burning and she could feel a small trickle actually running down her inner thigh provoking a small gasp of surprise. The books and the shop started to swirl around before her eyes, as did the vision of the man.

He turned from the book, concern on his face. She was clearly in a flush, he said, even faint? It was the air in the shop, the dust. Apologies poured forth, she must sit down and rest. Fifine, with embarrassment, protested that she was fine, quite all right, not going to faint. He though swept these feeble protests aside and his arm now encircled her waist supporting her weight, as if to anticipate some possible weakness or a sudden collapse. Innocently it seemed, his fingers touched the side of her breast and she felt her nipples harden in response to this intimacy. His physical closeness was overwhelming, his touch, his strength. Her token protests abated and she let him guide her to the rear of the shop, skirting piles of books and towering, dark shelves. He paused only to open a brown, varnished door, whereupon he moved behind her and both his hands took her by the slim waist as she was passed through.

They had entered a new world, a transformation that widened Fifine's eyes with their surprise. It was a large, high-ceilinged room, decorated with stucco plasterwork, every wall it seemed was covered in ornate, cut glass mirrors. Polished side tables supported vases, decanters and bowls in facetted glass and in the centre of the room soft, worn sofas were placed upon a sprawling Persian carpet. The glass was set into a fire of sparkling light by the thousands of beams thrown by the gas lit chandelier that hung magnificently from the plaster rose on the ceiling. Fifine had seen nothing like this extravagant display and her head almost whirled with amazement as he escorted her to a divan, but before she could sit down, her attention was suddenly taken by the vision of an immense bed, its proportions filling one end of the room like an altar.

It was a construction entirely of brass and glass. Intricately mated with the fluted brass tubes were cut glass columns and in the head and foot, glass sunbursts sent out cascades of fractured light. Covering its surface was a single sheet of rich, black velvet like a sea of nothingness. Over the bed, suspended on chains from the high ceiling was a walnut-framed mirror that reflected the entirety of the bed beneath it.

Having seated Fifine on the divan, the man disappeared through another door and returned shortly with a decanter and two crystal glasses. Working upon a side table, he carefully filled each glass with white wine and came and to sit beside her, offering her a glass.

"It's chilled and will help you to revive. Nothing better I can assure you."

She carefully accepted the glass and feeling his gaze watching her every move, equally carefully brought it to her lips and took a sip. The cold, fruity taste felt quite lovely and she again drank, this time a more substantial mouthful. She was smiling, returning his soft, playful smile. After a drink from his own glass he spoke again.

"There, you are looking so much improved already. I told you there was nothing better."

So they sat there. Quite formally and primly. He started to explain, with real enthusiasm, his great love of glass. Some, it seemed, he had inherited, and some he had collected from the many junk shops and flea markets in the city. Finally, as though he suddenly realised the need for it, he stopped and asked Fifine her name. He repeated it back to her several times, each time giving it a new sound and importance by changing the inflection in his voice. To Fifine this was wonderful.

"Mine is Paul," he finally told her. "Quite ordinary compared with yours."

Again, Fifine felt the redness rising through her shoulders to her face and lowered her head with embarrassment. To compensate she nervously finished her wine and Paul took her glass and refilled it. Their conversation grew bolder, the wine helping Fifine to become confident as Paul's eyes shone like the glass he loved. He said little things that of course made her laugh and at one moment, just when she was so very happy, he suddenly became serious. With a soft deliberation he told her that he thought she was a very beautiful girl and with hardly a moment given for this to take effect he moved to be beside her.

Fifine knew that she should perhaps react, perhaps move further up the divan? Get up, protest, or even leave? But this man was so different, compelling, 'dangerously' safe. She had after all let it happen, deep down wanted it to happen, yet her innocence of such things did not prepare her for this in any way. With the same presumption, he took her head in his hands, the same hands that had parted the pages of poetry and she watched his lips move inexorably towards her own full and parted mouth. Their mouths touched again and again, slowly, tentatively at first, little pecks of kisses. His tongue came out and instinctively she opened her mouth to receive it, letting in, letting herself be penetrated by this Paul. It was strong and searching, an utterly new experience for Fifine. It took command of her own tongue that retreated and submitted. A distinct wetness came again between her legs, together with that insatiable fire. His mouth at times left hers to probe her long neck. She felt her bosom swell and tingle as her breathing became halting and rapid. A desire to submit to this man, to her own feelings, overwhelmed all else.

He lifted her by the arms and led her to the area of the great bed, up so dangerously close to it, the size and splendour filling her view. He turned to face her and asked, in an almost clandestine whisper, if she would like to undress for him.

"Undress," he repeated. "Just as you would at home. As though I were not here. You are so beautiful, so much more beautiful than all of this." His hand took in the crystal room. "It is but a frame for your beauty and it will give me such pleasure just to watch you."

He let her go and moved to sit upon the edge of the bed, compressing the springs with his weight. For Fifine it was as though the request had no solution but to comply. All her commonsense, her natural reticence had left her and she desperately wanted to please Paul. Above all to let him see her body for she had never had such intimate attention nor such clear adoration in her sheltered life.

So, in answer, she moved a few feet from him and as he had suggested imagined that she was alone at her aunt's house and undressing in the privacy of her bedroom. Her hands moved first to the buttons of her crisp blouse. Her mind paid attention to the task, nimble fingers going smoothly from button to button until the garment was undone to her small waist. Then she undid the leather waist belt and the buttons at the side of her skirt, released, its folds slipped soundlessly to the floor. She paused for a moment standing there in her knee length, white knickers, black wool stockings and laced ankle boots.

Paul took this all in watching from where he sat. He could

clearly see that where her mound swelled at her crutch, where the material was drawn a little tight, that it was also dark with her moisture. Fifine undid the neat row of buttons at each wrist and with a wriggle of her shoulders let the blouse fall to the floor. The upper half of her young body was now only covered by a simple lace-edged bodice, held at the front by a little row of pink ribbons. A deep, dark cleavage ran down to where the breasts beneath pushed out the material, its lacy thinness hiding little of the points driving out.

Ribbon by ribbon, now with heightened slowness, she pulled each bow free. The last one undone Fifine shrugged the bodice from her. Paul could not stifle a deep murmur of approval and at this sound she became again aware of his presence. For a moment she was embarrassed but the look of sincere pleasure across his face reassured and encouraged Fifine. Somewhere, with a natural modesty, and even more natural female insecurity, Fifine had been concerned that what she had, what she was, beneath her clothing would fall short of his expectations of her. The appreciation of her audience emboldened her and with an unusual wantonness she let her hands push her breasts up from below, her long, delicate fingers lifting the dark areolas to point upwards and towards him.

Fifine sensed a strange power filling her, a power that came from the possession of her body and its obvious effect upon Paul. She stooped, arching her back so that the spine showed clearly through the white skin and her bosom hung towards the ground. Then with care she unlaced and removed each boot. In this action, she had half turned away from Paul and the perfect form of her desirable bottom stretched the fabric of the knickers across the globes so tightly, it was as if they were uncovered. Paul stirred restlessly at this display, his composure for a moment disturbed.

This was further disturbed as she looked back at him with her sweet face, the curls of her hair catching the light and her eyes, dark and highlighted by pin pricks of reflection.

Standing again, the drawstring of the knickers was undone and with a little provocative series of inevitable movements she pulled them down and off each leg. Now only the plain black stocking with cheeky red garters remained and Paul found that the way that they framed her crutch was completely entrancing.

"Leave them on Fifine, please leave the stockings on." His voice was warm and rich laden with approval. "They seem to accentuate your legs, to perhaps enshrine that darkness of curls that lies above. You are all black below and so perfectly white above, except of course for the deep rich, pink at the ends of your breasts. You are so beautiful."

Again this word 'beautiful' made Fifine tremble as did these extraordinary descriptions of her appearance. She felt an appreciation that transcended everything. The city, her aunt, her smelly job, all seemed so very far in her past. This was a moment that even her girl's vivid dreams and imagination had never conjured.

Paul stood up and took her hand in his and made a gesture towards the bed.

"Will you please me so much further? Will you lie down upon the bed?" he asked.

Fifine smiled and asked how she should do that, how he would like her to do that. She was eager to please, eager not to appear gauche or to make a mistake and destroy the spell that was upon her.

"In the middle, on your back. Right in the middle, your head upon the bolster beneath the velvet."

He watched as she climbed on, showing little details of her

private places. She settled herself down as he had instructed and the black velvet beneath her skin felt cool and soothing. Paul moved to the foot of the bed and looked over its rail, directly down upon Fifine.

"Spread your legs wide and stretch your arms outward above your head, like a magnificent star fish on the sand of a beach. Fifine devoid of embarrassment or coyness about exposing so openly her sex, did as she was asked and looking up she indeed saw herself like a star fish in a black heaven, her black stockinged legs from the white thighs downward almost invisible against the velvet except for the flash of red from the garters. Above all, just as Paul also saw, she could spy the sweet pink, opened lips of her sex, still with no more than a youthful dab of curls upon the mound, open and glistening.

It was upon this essential place that Paul's eyes focused. The way that the opened lips gleamed from the mirrored light. It drew his thoughts within, tempting and enticing his mind and his will. Still transfixed and staring, Paul at last asked Fifine in a soft voice if she had ever been with a man before? She answered, almost provocatively, that he would be the first. In one moment both making an assumption that the possibility, of such an act taking place between them, was no longer a question still to be resolved.

Fifine had no real understanding of what might be entailed in the undertaking of such a secret and never-discussed union. She was aware that this was the mysterious and guarded place of the adult world that no one had ever shared with her in any detail and, with the determination that some women seem to possess, she would wait to discover no further. This would, as she saw it in her mind, be the moment. Paul moved from her view and she could hear the sounds of undressing. She still remained spread beneath the mirror, reluctant to do anything, at least not without clear instruction. She had never seen a man naked. Boys in her village, bathing in the river with their small, sweet organs yes but never a real man.

Paul, suddenly appeared in her line of vision, reflected by the wall mirrors on all sides. He moved to be beside the bed. Fifine stared. Paul was now a strange and compelling sight. His body was lean and muscular, a little dark hair crowned his chest between his small nipples. Little traces of hair trickled down his abdomen to finish at a place upon which her eyes focused. Fifine though was suddenly aware that he held in his hands, a length of what seemed to be white silken cord. She was still mesmerised by the force of the moment and even as he started without explanation to secure her ankle to the bed she made no attempt at protest. He continued to tie her to the corners of the bed, walking around, first ankles then her unprotesting wrists. Always he held her eyes with his as though to reassure her. He was gentle as he wound the cords around her limbs, but when she came to test them she could hardly move. She wanted to question this disturbing development but the restraints seemed, in a strange way, to subdue her so she kept quiet.

Finished, Paul climbed up onto the bed and took up his position upon his knees between her exceptionally parted thighs. With great delicacy the fingers of his hand now explored Fifine's offered sex. Always he continued to hold her gaze, as though watching her face and expressions so as to guide his fingers work. Already dizzy with her arousal, Fifine could do nothing but succumb to these extraordinary attentions. Sensations beyond any experience seemed to burn through her. Starting between her legs they expanded and washed in endless waves through her system. At times it was all too much and her mouth opened to gasp and cry out in an attempt to relieve the tensions. As these unbearable pleasures gripped her she twisted and strained against the cords, so tightening the bindings even to the point of pain. Paul was slow and most methodical, using his skills with the precision of a craftsman. Step by glorious step, he moved the girl up to reach at last, her point of climax. As she came, she tore at the bonds and drove her pelvis into his hand, shouting and crying out his name.

Even as Fifine's mind glazed over with the experience of her first orgasm, so Paul altered his position and guided himself into her. A momentary look of horror swept across Fifine's face as she felt herself so opened. She cried out again, in pain, as he forced himself in, and then she was calm again, as he lay above her, supporting his weight and gently kissing her sweating face. Fifine felt so strange, so beautiful, so filled. Equally gently he started to move inside her, whispering and soothing her with soft sounds and words of encouragement till she found her second orgasm. This time her mouth opened in a silent scream and beads of sweat between her twisting breasts, caught at the light.

However Paul was not finished. He climbed from her without pause and loosed the ropes that held her ankles. Dexterously he tied these cords to the same posts of the brass bed that held her wrists. Fifine was exquisitely but so indecently folded and exposed, her bottom lifted clear of the black velvet and her other hole clearly on show. Paul wetted himself with her freely flowing juices and entered her there with as much tenderness as he could muster. Nevertheless, at first she cried out as a searing pain, even panic, engulfed her, but as he used her there one hand comforted Fifine by stroking her head and slipping its fingers into her open mouth.

Slowly the discomfort turned to a new and demanding pleasure and she willingly again accepted the man, looking up with awe as he arched above her trembling body. It was in this place that Paul at last permitted himself to release. They were both now soaked in sweat in the warmth of the room. Finally he withdrew and sat back on his heels, then with great precision set about methodically slapping the tight flesh of her round bottom with his hand, a number of times to each cheek. As his palm made contact Fifine emitted a surprised cry for he was in no way gentle. The last smack surprised and hurt her most for it landed directly upon her vulva. Strange and surprising as this action was, she found it reassuring and even pleasant, the stinging it left behind, especially between her legs, stimulated her afresh. With a familiar tousling of her hair, he slipped from the bed and set about undoing the ropes but still leaving them attached to her limbs. She, relieved of her stressful position, curled up upon on her side quite exhausted. He left her and returned shortly with freshly filled glasses of wine. He gently held up her head and placed a glass to her lips while she drank. This done, he wiped her forehead with a handkerchief and gently pulled the velvet cover over her.

At their subsequent meetings they played and developed many games and variations. They explored the cracks and crevices of each other's bodies, Fifine always growing bolder and more curious about the man and his fascinating body. When Fifine was provocative and teasing, Paul would sometimes let her wriggle happily across his knee while he sat upon a couch and used his hand on her bare bottom. When they romped upon the darkness of the velvet, she would like to open her legs and let his hand again descend and bring a burning fire to that sensitive place that would then need quelling in other ways. But never again did the bed ever seem so big and overwhelming to Fifine, and never again did Paul tie her to its gleaming tubes, though she would often ask and beg. He would only laugh and say that it was only done to 'innocent girls', not to a woman like her. It pleased Fifine to think that she was now, in his eyes, a woman and when she stood naked in the centre of the room and the mirrors confirmed this to her. One great mirror, the one above the bed, showed her the writhing and twisting form of a 'strange' woman engulfed by pleasure, a woman who she could never truly believe was herself, a woman who had found the dangerous cocktail of first love. For how could this be the country girl that still lived deep within her, the one who still marvelled wide-eyed at the world of the city outside?

II THE DISCIPLINING OF SARAH JANE BALSTRODE

THE YELLOW GASLIGHT ILLUMINATED the polished brass handle of the heavy door that was before her. Her knock upon the oak board, though a most deliberately timid knock, was to her regret heard by her uncle, who in a firm voice bade her enter.

Her uncle's study was a place of order and function. Heavy and often consulted tomes were restrained in fluted shelves which covered most of the surfaces except that occupied by the large fireplace. The hissing, globed gas lights upon the walls warmed the room with their yellow glow; a coal oil lamp of complex design placed upon the working surface, lit both her uncle and his papers. Sarah Jane walked forward and positioned herself quite centrally before his large partners desk. The lean, cold man did not look up but instead, with studious attention, continued to write; inkwell to paper, back and forth, her eyes followed the moving hand, finding its rhythm quite hypnotic. Slowly the beat of the regulator clock intruded into the silence to join the scratch of the pen and she turn her head to become now absorbed by the regular flick of the seconds hand as it passed the time.

She was jerked back to attention from this temporary mesmeric state by her uncle's voice. It was obvious to him that she had entirely missed his opening words; so, slightly more laboured and certainly louder he repeated himself.

"This will not do, this will not do young lady; not do at all." As he said this he blotted his last writing with studied care and placed the pen in a rack.

"Dear, dear." At the second 'dear' the silver lid of the inkwell snapped down with a practised flick of his finger, as if to deliberately add punctuation.

Sarah Jane, sensing more from the tone than the words placed her hands behind her back and bowed her head submissively, which caused her curled ringlets of rich brown hair to charmingly hang forward. She dared not catch his eyes even though they were most consciously upon her.

"Miss Meltrose… a most diligent woman, a woman who has had the misfortune to have been your governess for many years, has, yet again, had cause to bring to my attention her concerns about your attitude and behaviour. This fine teacher, who has had the thankless task of providing your education and guiding your moral development, regretfully it seems, has reached the end of her quite extraordinary patience."

Her uncle paused to attempt to re-arrange his sheets more neatly than they already were. He guided his hands down each side of the sheets as though to square them, repeating the useless action a number of times.

"It appears, so I have been told and indeed seen with my own eyes the very evidence of injury, that you bit the arm of Miss Meltrose; *bit it*… young lady!" He waved a hand.

"Laid your teeth upon the very person of your esteemed Governess while she attempted to provide some most necessary and rightful discipline. In all my time as your Guardian, is this how you repay my generosity and devoted efforts to perform my duty in the matter of your guidance and upbringing? Is this how, young Miss?" His voice rose at the repeat of the question and Sarah Jane was drawn to look up and foolishly catch his eye.

"There!" he said, with almost triumph. "Such a wilful look,

such a flash of insolence, I am bemused that there should be such a wicked will in any girl and, God forbid, in a person of my blood and my dear Brother's blood. Where have we all failed and gone astray to find this contradiction of fine breeding before me?"

She was well aware that he was rapidly developing his most coldly controlled temper. For she had seen this progress many times before, stood as she was now, before this very desk as so many times before, listening as he now explained again her shortcomings in ever more expressive detail. She equally knew the eventual outcome of such a tirade, so to make a limit upon the damage already done she kept her head bowed and strove hard for an appearance, at least, of abject contrition.

Her uncle, never to be cheated of his moment, droned on, expanding, sometimes even with theatrical eloquence, the litany of the faults of Sarah Jane. At one moment there was justifiable anger, the next the long sighs of exasperation, even capitulation, as though no solution would ever come to his much-troubled mind. At last she heard him say the long awaited but disturbing words...

"There is no solution other than to ring for Mrs. Wixon, no solution my girl, none indeed but Mrs. Wixon." he said this as though Mrs. Wixon was some panacea for all his ills, to be delivered like a medicinal draught.

Mrs. Wixon though was as far from a healing draught as one could get; for she was as cold a body as Sarah Jane's uncle, each for this reason alone, quite suited to the temperament of the other. As housekeeper to her uncle, the other servants and even the governess Miss Meltrose, were fearful of this tall, gaunt lady who found fault with most things and threatened dismissal often. It was known that in her private realm below stairs, she soundly whipped and birched the young maids, who accepted such practice rather than face the alternative of the street without reference. Not only was Mrs. Wixon keeper of her uncle's human property but she was the extension of her uncle's will in many different ways. As far as Sarah Jane was concerned she constantly reported to the Master, the details of every transgression, perceived or real, that the Ward perpetrated within the house and, when her uncle deemed it necessary for Sarah Jane's' punishment, she was his arm in this matter too.

"Go on girl do as you are told, apply yourself to the bell."

Sarah Jane roused herself from her submissive posture and crossed the room to work the handle by the mantle piece. She was well aware that the bell would find Mrs. Wixon seated in the warmth of the kitchen, she also knew that Mrs. Wixon would of course be waiting for the harsh jangle of the bell, undoubtedly forewarned that her services would shortly be needed.

"When the good Mrs. Wixon has performed her sorry duties with you," her uncle anticipated, "there will be, I hope, a reformed young lady, set upon a course of good behaviour; at least that is what I perhaps foolishly expect."

The knock upon the door and instruction to enter brought the arrival of the housekeeper to the scene. Sarah Jane's uncle appeared to take some deep pleasure in the ritual that was to follow. Uncle and housekeeper, observed the requirements of discussion and explanation as though for each the inevitable end was some new surprise. Yet as Sarah Jane knew only too well, the charade was played out as often as twice or more each month and had been since she had been taken in by her kindly Patron some many years ago, upon the untimely death, by fatal accident, of her parents. The only unknown that she had as a surprise would be the severity of her punishment; this was usually arrived at by a means of barter as though her suffering was the price of potatoes in a market.

At last, as some relief from waiting for the poor girl, Mrs. Wixon was asked to bring forth the instrument of instruction from it hiding place lying upon a row of books. Whereas her Governess had relied ineffectually upon a small bundle of twigs tied with blue ribbon, her uncle had chosen a most serious length of rattan, almost the thickness of a little finger and flexible enough to bent into a circle. Though his choice for his Ward, it was always Mrs. Wixon who applied it, for he, it seemed, preferred to watch.

"Now Miss. said Mrs. Wixon in a dry voice. "May I ask you to prepare in the usual way for me to undertake the Master's will?"

Sarah Jane now moved to her task. To one side of the study was an unusual chair, chosen, she was sure, specifically for the needs of her discipline. It was a period chair of a design from an earlier time. A semi-circle of wood, arms and seat all one, set upon stout splayed legs. While the two watched in silence Sarah Jane, with some effort, moved the chair to the centre of the room. Satisfied with its correct positioning, she then without further bidding reached down and gathered up both her dress and petticoats. With a practised movement, she held the clothing up above her waist so exposing her long white cotton knickers that ended with a lace trim at the junction with her laced ankle boots.

How many gentlemen would have paid guinea to see such a sweet mature young maid so revealed? Instead it was her uncle who enjoyed the sight for free. However, still more revelations to shatter her modesty were still required. Still holding up her clothes, with some difficulty she laid herself with her stomach down upon the seat of the chair. This conveniently, pinched the dress and petticoats in their raised place. Sarah Jane now wriggled forward so that her breasts, arms and head were well over the far side of the seat, the high sides, keeping her arms held forward at the shoulder.

At a perfunctory nod from Sarah Jane's uncle, Mrs. Wixon now moved to her work. She rested the long cane across the arms of the chair and set about exposing the place of punishment. The knickers, divided as they were into two separate legs, were pulled open at the division and tucked hard at the sides to prevent their closing. The naked, round, full orbs of the girl's bottom were nicely exposed. Each cheek rose up to catch the light, and the deep cleft between was dark and mysterious.

At a barley polite instruction from Mrs. Wixon Sarah Jane, opened her legs wide, balancing upon the toes of her boots to better steady the posture, this, inevitably insuring that her ripe sex, trimmed with dark curls, was now on show, especially to the vantage point of her uncle.

"You know not to alter your position and to keep your noises quiet Miss?" explained Mrs. Wixon.

"Or, else I'm sure the Master will be adding further strokes for your disobedience."

She then turned to him, cane in hand once more. "What, sir, will be your pleasure for the young Miss?"

"Ah my good Mrs. Wixon, there we have the problem. I am, as you are most aware, a kind-hearted soul when it comes to the matter of such necessary discipline, such as is necessitated by my niece's constant, errant behaviour. It was a most serious incident and if I said but a dozen, I'm sure that such a girl, with a bottom so frequently used to the strokes, would shrug them off with indifference and be laughing behind our backs in no time."

"With respect Sir," Mrs. Wixon interjected, "a maturing and most firm pair of cheeks, such as the young Miss has and noting their regular acquaintance and experience with this instrument, would hardly discern, as you have wisely observed, its attentions if it be but a dozen." She paused, as if with intense deliberation.

"The incident as you have explained – *biting* to be sure! – needs such a tendency curbing in any girl. More than her normal six, more even than a sterner dozen. May I make so bold as to suggest that as the young Miss has not yet been educated by the rod upon the backs of her thighs that we take this opportunity to instruct her to this common and effective practice? I know from much experience of the delinquency of young girls, that the tenderness of this area breaks a wilful spirit something proper. We could Sir, if I may suggest, let Miss Sarah Jane, taste six upon each thigh and a dozen well placed upon her most challenging, firm, behind?"

"Now where would I be without your common sense and experience Mrs. Wixon?" asked the Master.

"A bachelor such as I am knows nothing of the punishment of a quite wicked female; I'm sure your long experience of the disciplining of house girls leaves you in good stead. My niece has certainly fought against the traces of respectable behaviour and if you feel that your prescription is a suitable remedy, then my kindly nature must be overruled by your wise council. Let it be as you say, good lady."

Things now took an unusual turn for Sarah Jane. Mrs. Wixon's sadistic suggestion had made the girl's stomach tighten with fear. She had steeled herself for twelve or even eighteen on her experienced behind, such a dose was bad but equally she could pace herself for those strokes. What was mentioned and now to be applied to her thighs, it seemed, held the terrors of the unknown.

She therefore slowly responded in something of a trance to the instructions of the housekeeper. First she had to stand again while still holding up her dress, to permit the string at the top of her knickers to be undone and the cotton fabric, briskly pulled down.

The gartered stockings were now also pulled into concertinas below the knees. This left her naked from the waist down, her neat triangle of hair crowning her mound above the long white thighs, all clearly on show as further treat before her uncle.

True embarrassment made her hang her head, yet there was though no time for that display of contrition for she was soon bade again to lay over the chair and part her legs to the maximum that her rolled down knickers allowed. Though this was still not enough parting for the meticulous Mrs. Wixon, who knelt down upon the carpet and with some difficulty worked one frilly leg of the draws right over and off the boot. Then with her own hands she spread the girl's legs indecently wide open.

"Unless you are foolish, you will keep those legs still and where I have put them till the matter's over." Mrs. Wixon calmly pointed out. Sarah Jane knew well what was meant by 'foolish'.

The gas lights aided by the desk lamp had no trouble now in illuminating the round bottom and the gaping moist sex beneath. As the expanse of pale thighs ran outward from the bottom the skin of their backs tightened as the muscles strove to keep the legs out straight. Mrs. Wixon spent time finding the ideal position. At each adjustment she tapped the last few inches of the cane upon the target area of youthful skin. Her cruelty knew the ideal place, just below the sharp line of the base of the cheeks with the cane well angled so that it would be more upon the inside of the thigh and quite deliberately, frighteningly close to the pouting virgin lips.

Methodically she pulled back her white-cuffed sleeve to the elbow and re-gripped the shaft of the cane. Then, after al the anticipation of the involved preparations, it finally rose up and behind her head, paused, only to descend with a savage whip of the arm. The air whistled with its passage and the rattan was halted, with a cunning back flip of the wrist so producing a sharp crack as it found its tender mark. Sarah Jane's whole body seemed to shudder in response, a vibration of intense agony gripping it, as a gasping cry broke from her open mouth.

Mrs. Wixon pronounced a simple 'one'. After a lengthy pause, the arm rose to repeat the strike. Even before the arm had fallen again, the skin of beautiful thigh had risen up in a deep, double tracked, red weal where the fury of the springy cane had been applied.

The chastisement continued. Each stroke was duly numbered and each stroke caused Sarah Jane to cry out a little and shudder as the dreadful pain vibrated through her every sinew. By 'four', some strokes had deliberately returned to the exact site of a previous mark and small red beads of blood, oozing from the tortured flesh, rewarded these cruel returns.

At 'six' there was a pause to allow Mrs. Wixon to move to the other side and address the girl's unpunished thigh. Sarah Jane was moved, more than once, to plead for a stop to the beating, her voice broken by sobs, tinged now with some genuine contrition. The one watching with voyeuristic intensity and the one performing the act, had though no intention of being moved to mercy and the useless pleas served only to fuel their individual, secret delights.

Even when no stroke was actually applied, Sarah Jane's body shook and her knees to tremble, due to the effect upon the nerves so close to the skin in that area. The punishment of the other thigh, with some strokes actually moving aside the strands of her intimate hair, so close did they fly near her crutch, was too much for the uncle's niece, it seemed. For at last she could no longer support her legs straight out, so at the third on that thigh, she collapsed onto her knees quite distraught. This change from the orthodox posture required for this beating caused the Housekeeper to pause in her delivery exhibiting much annoyance.

"You see, Sir?" she exclaimed, sounding almost hurt.

"Even during the most serious moment of her punishment the young Miss cannot display any discipline. When she has composed herself, I suggest we add another six to the dozen for her bottom and more if she should so defy your good self again."

"You are so correct, Mrs. Wixon. Though painful I'm sure, I fear there are histrionics at work here to gain our sympathy and moderate your arm. Get my ward to return to the formal position so the matter of her thighs can be concluded and her most provocative bottom, twisting as it so does, take its now eighteen."

Sarah Jane's uncle seemed by now to have lost his detachment and be instead, quite involved with the bodily movements of his finely exposed Ward.

Mrs. Wixon, well used to the games and ploys of the youthful female when caned, placed her mouth close to the ear of the girl and explained most clearly that the tally would continue to rise should she not have her thighs out straight and parted well in a very trice. Sarah Jane, though experiencing pain as she had never known it before, was sensible enough to the sincerity of the threats, and therefore with great effort of will, pulled herself up and stretched out her legs again to receive the last three dreadful cuts on such a sensitive place. Mrs. Wixon was in no hurry to help the girl past this difficult moment and again went though her own careful positioning, so that when the cane at last came down it was most accurately laid upon the criss-cross of existing lines. The next and the last followed, again drawing a little blood.

Knowing that some tightening of the posterior's flesh would help to emphasis the sensations, she commanded the girl to now draw her knees up to the chair and push out her bottom. Slowly and painfully this change of posture was achieved there still being much involuntary shaking of the lower half. The bottom so presented, filled and swelled as the naked, unblemished skin tightened. Mrs. Wixon adjusted her stance to a more lateral swing and the rattan fairly wined as it passed through the air to leave the characteristic, beautiful, double tracked line across the centres of the rounded cheeks. Perhaps there was more force or perhaps the girl had been truly broken but this first stroke drew an uncontrolled wail from Sarah Jane.

" Hush your noise, young Miss." advised the Housekeeper. "A young woman as you are now, shows her breeding and maturity, she holds her tongue when she bends for punishment. More of that and I'm sure that the Master will be adding strokes for the annoyance to his delicate ear by the volume of your silly whines."

It was as if from then on Mrs. Wixon was quite bent upon the challenge of drawing another wilful shriek. The strokes were at her full and not inconsiderable strength. The eighteen worked closely together, concentrating the agony and soon drawing the essential blood, seen always as a testimony of the thoroughness of the application. Though her bottom clenched and opened in an involuntary rhythm, Sarah Jane was at least used to this form of pain of which her sweet behind had so many memories. So it was that only small, restrained gasps and little moans passed her panting lips to signify the contact of each burning cut.

At the end, Mrs. Wixon, ordered her victim to get up and stand before her uncle. Poor Sarah Jane did this with much difficulty, wedged as she was between the arms of the chair and hampered by the continuing spasms of her freshly abused lower half. At last she stood. Bemused as she was, Sarah Jane was still very careful to keep her garments up and clear of the streaks of blood, least she should stain her clothes and earn another visit. Her knickers, still hung untidily from one ankle and tears stained her face. Dishevelled and contrite, she was past caring about the nudity of her lower half before her uncle.

"As always, you have performed your difficult duties with diligence, Mrs. Wixon. I am most grateful. Please return the instrument and leave me with my niece, for I have matters to instruct her in."

Mrs. Wixon, produced a small cloth from her pocket and wiped the length of the cane, then returned it to its sinister home upon the book shelf. She rolled back her sleeve and, with a polite nod of her head, left the room. Sarah Jane, swayed slightly before the desk, her clothes still grimly gathered up. Her uncle was roused as he had never been before, perhaps for the first time looking upon his niece as the young woman she really was and not just a naughty girl. He was beyond himself with desire, his member hard within his trousers.

It is therefore quite possible he did submit to his inflamed lusts and indeed penetrate his niece, having her bend at his desk and perhaps taking her from behind. He was ignorant of the female sex but aware of the risks of pregnancy and the obvious blood that would indicate the loss of her virginity. He had learnt this other way at school, tight and pleasurable, one that would safely sate his thirst. The loyal Mrs Wixon, had loitered beyond the closed door and she did it seems, clearly hear the girl produce a different but clear series of cries. The cruel Mrs Wixon would never know. After all, the cries may have resulted from the girl being bent over his desk and the Master's hand performing a detailed and uncomfortable examination of Sarah Jane's marked bottom. That must remain a mystery for now, perhaps to be unfolded in another story...

III   THE PARIS CRAFTSMAN

THE RUE DE L'ENTRANCE was to be found on the southern edge of the great city of Paris. It was an unimportant street of small, dilapidated houses long past their best, if they had ever had a best. Cats sat on hot stones to drink of the noonday sun and a midday silence more suited to a small village lay over the area. Alison parked her small red sports car as near to the building she sought as possible. She crossed the road to the paint-peeled door marked with a blue enamel number nine. After hesitating, she knocked hard and waited. There was a long pause, and she had just raised her hand to knock again, when she heard a noise from within. The man who opened the door to her was short, bent, old and foreign.

"Herr Grossman?" she enquired in English.

He nodded through half glasses.

"Alison Kwik," she said, extending a hand which he did not take. "Come in," he said in a thick German accent. He led her into a dark and dirty hall. Instantly the cool air was full of the smell of leather, stacked along the walls were large rolled hides in many colours and ahead was a narrow staircase, equally ill lit. The old man went ahead and up the stairs and she followed. At the top he disappeared through a half opened door into a strange and crowded room. It was at the rear of the building and light flooded in through a large, dust-encrusted skylight. All around were cluttered work benches covered in strips of leather and gleaming tools polished with their constant use. The sweet smell of leather hung heavily in the air, full of sensual animal power.

Herr Grossman had by now seated himself in a position of power against the light.

"So you have come for one of my little toys?" He asked, his eyes sparkling with an excitement not suggested by this age. Alison agreed with him, feeling both embarrassed and excited by the situation she found herself in. Though there was still a strong hint of the active male in the old man, there was also the professional detachment that all specialists cultivate. With the ease of long experience and complete familiarity with the difficulties almost all his clients found with the situation for the first time, he launched into his familiar routine. First he seated her by pointing to the only other chair in the room, then with delight, he started to describe his service in detail.

"We could have a half harness but that would not be for someone as beautiful and so well created by nature as you. No, for you," - here he paused to give effect to his consideration - "No, for you, a full and very elaborate harness is the only suitable one. You are fit and young and yours would be a perfect body for something so wonderful and so... demanding.

"Now," he paused again, holding his chin with his hand, "we must consider the most important of design decisions. Will you require a female as well as a male extension?" Before Alison could even begin to answer, he answered for her.

"Yes, again you are someone who will most definitely want a female extension, that is... personally internal; if you don't mind me being blunt. We will have to consider both size and shape.... in fact to do this correctly and to give you my very best work, I must be permitted to measure everything."

He held up his hand to suggest protection or reassurance. "My clients trust me, and I am sure that you will be no different. I have been recommended to you and for me to do my best for you, we must trust each other."

At this point Alison felt that she had better say something.

"Herr Grossman, I would not be here unless I was willing to undertake what is necessary to possess an example of your extraordinary skill. I will, of course, be only too pleased to co-operate with you to achieve this."

"Good, good, we understand each other. Then we must get on. I regret, my facilities are very limited," he gestured around the room. "May I ask you to remove all your clothing? While you do this, I will get some things together so that I can take my measurements."

Alison found the moment and the request most stimulating. This was certainly no doctor's surgery but the same detached pressure to conform was there and keenly felt. She had undressed in front of many men but this was hardly that — more like a dressmaker but even then... different.

Herr Grossman turned away and started to gather together a number of obviously essential items. Alison set about undressing. Fortunately, she had on only casual clothes. First she looked around to find a place to put them. Seeing nothing obvious, she opted for the already crowded bench. With slightly false confidence, she pulled the tight cashmere sweater over her head. The expensively soft material rubbed gently over her hardened nipples, teasing them further, for she seldom wore a bra. The cool air of the room felt fresh on her bared breasts. They delighted her and also those who were allowed to play with them, male or female. Hard, high and very round, they were a little larger than her slim, long frame dictated. Their ends were dark with the areola distended, developed, she felt, by the work of mouths upon them. Next she methodically unlaced her high-heeled boots, pulled them off and placed them neatly under the bench.

She had to stand to remove her skin tight jeans. She pulled them down her long legs with difficulty and had to hop to keep her balance. She was left with her small plain thong, the cord at the back disappearing between her round, firm buttocks, the thin material at the front cupping the noticeably distended mound, moist where it slipped between the slightly parted lips.

The progress of the undressing had not escaped the alert eyes of Herr Grossman, "Everything, please, young lady, everything.", He made a slight movement of his hands and Alison looked down at her brief white covering and the pink pop socks.

"You can leave the socks on," said Herr Grossman; as though such a concession would ensure her modesty. Alison slipped her thumbs through the thin elastic and in one movement pushed the thong down to her feet, where she kicked it free. She stood up, legs slightly parted, to confront Herr Grossman with the closely trimmed and most minimal crowning of pubic hair over the powerfully displayed generous mound and the fully depilated, lustful mouth formed by her labia.

"Few," said Herr Grossman, "of my many clients could be considered more worthy an owner of my talents than you." His eyes shone and his face beamed with the obvious appreciation of a connoisseur; one who in the course of his work must have seen so many female bodies. Alison always liked a compliment, and smiled shyly back at him.

"Now to work. First we will measure the female requirement."

He turned back to his bench and picked up a beautiful veneered box bound with brass corners. This he placed on a table and with care raised the lid. The long box was lined with dark blue velvet and held, in individual compartments, perhaps a dozen beautifully shaped red leather dildos in ascending order of size. Herr Grossman repeated this display with another identical box. This, however, contained similar objects that differed only in having exaggerated heads at their ends.

"We have, young lady, two choices in this department. First that of size or length and then between the type of even diameter and the type with the full head, mimicking, even exaggerating upon, the natural form. For those who have, shall we say, a problem with arousal, I can make special shafts which have uncomfortable ridges. I doubt though," said he, again making decisions for her, "that you would have a problem there? The only way to choose is to try, otherwise I have found that sometimes a woman's eyes are bigger than, shall we say her, stomach. May I also hasten to assure you that though these samples have experienced many… eh… trials, they are always cleansed most thoroughly with surgical spirit. The leather from which they are made, and from which the one I make for you will be made, is of the finest quality, as soft as the place it must enter and yet almost totally waterproof. I fill the sheath with my own preparation, which permits some flexibility and feels most natural. You may also consider if you require a device to only fill the vagina, or to be more dramatic, even painfully demanding and pass through the mouth of the cervix and beyond. To fill or be fully filled? You may also have one fitted, of a suitable design, to enter your rear passage well."

Alison was by now very wet and very open. This almost clinical talk on such an erotic theme was deeply stimulating.

Her hole, in fact holes, now craved to be filled by the superb objects that she saw laid out so invitingly before her. It was like a sweet shop and she a child with pennies to spend. What to try first?

"I think I would like a head on the item, of a size I would notice, and I think that I would like one for my bum as well.

You would know how best it would be shaped for there." She hesitated, her hand hovering over the, boxes.

"Take one," encouraged Herr Grossman.

Her hand reached out and moved over the box, back and forth. Then with decision, it alighted upon and removed a substantial dildo. Its leather was so inviting, warm to the touch and softer even than her cashmere. She brought it instinctively to her nose and breathed deeply of its rich, carnal smell. Her mind also visualized the pink, wet and open slits that this had already entered and she noticeably trembled at the thought of driving this hard monster in; pushing and twisting it as the willing recipient thrust back and writhed, skewered upon its insatiable attack. She moved it away from her nose, and as it passed her month her tongue licked out to caress the large, round, impossible end.

Now oblivious of Herr Grossman, and yet aroused by the audience he generated, she brought its head down to meet her own cunt. To make the entry possible she instinctively arched her hips forward, bending and opening her legs. This movement had the effect of parting her swollen lips, and as she drew the soft leather between them for the first time, letting the liquids wet it, pausing to caress; the need to plunge it in became very strong. Still, as though in a greeting, she let it rub against her now erect clitoris and this touch sent its own uniquely female messages throughout her body.

Then it was in. At first she felt that she had been too greedy. As her hand and arm, beyond her control, forced it in and upward, she felt herself stretched as she had never been stretched before. She could feel it pass the inner gate with just a little pleasant pain, and then it was onward. Her whole self filled with a wonderful glow, like some silk gloved fist had driven home, punishment and pleasure washed together. As only the last few inches of the massive device were left as a bright red circle framed in the engorged mouth, she was aware again of Herr Grossman close by her.

"May I make some checks, young lady?" be said in his professional voice, seemingly oblivious to her experience.

"Yes," agreed Alison, her voice braking. He bent his head as she held her position standing thrust forward with her legs well parted. She felt his hand touching and testing, then his skilled craftsman's fingers sliding between the dildo and, incredibly, the wall of her vagina, increasing the stretch significantly, finding even more from her young ring. Then the fingers were withdrawn and the hand moved with now moist fingers up over her mound to the area of her womb. Here it pressed, just above the pubic bone. She was aware of his other hand on the end of the dildo and then its movement of the device; so that it pushed out hard against her skin. Still holding her in this way he looked up at her face.

"If you were an adventurous girl, you could in my considered opinion, get the greatest pleasure from the next size up. You are young and very accommodating... elastic. This one you would soon become comfortable with use, the next size would always provide a challenge."

Without waiting for an answer, he gently pulled the dildo from her body with little twisting

motions that thrilled her. Accepting that the matter had already been decided, he turned and placed the used dildo, now wet and gleaming, on a sheet of plastic and selected the next in line. There was a decided jump in the increments of size and this one looked quite amazing – more a device of torture than of pleasure.

He handed it To Alison. "Go on, you will learn to enjoy it...... even worship it. I know these things; it is my trade to know women's needs... I always know."

Alison took it and tried not to look. She knew that this too had been elsewhere and if another had been able to accept it then she would not be beaten and not admit defeat in front of this arrogant old man. It was worse and there was pain, like the first moments of being taken in her arse, but she had never contemplated the incredible feeling of being filled in this way; she could not restrain a gasp. But she had not made this journey to this place, to this old man, to find anything less than the total experience. This was an essential part of it, this size was to be hers. There were even larger ones in the box. Who they were for she dared not think. She pushed the last few inches hard, almost staggering against the fire that nearly made her come. Herr Grossman again went through his methodical examination. She cried out a little as his fingers distended, probed and evaluated.

"This is yours my dear, of this there is no doubt. In the future, when you are in your private world, you will thank me."

Alison believed, clearly, that she would. She sat back on the chair after removing the monster, to regain something of her composure. The old man searched for another item and at last produced a tube of proprietary genital lubricant. He now selected a red dildo this one was quite small and handed it to Alison.

"For the other hole, it is better that it is not too large, so that it can move freely as your body moves; this will give much more… sensation. See, it has a special waist, to permit your tight muscle to lock around it."

He passed her the tube, and she anointed the bulbous shaft with gel, and, standing up again, she bent forward so that she could reach and insert it, bending, almost double to spread her cheeks.

"Don't lose it," cautioned Herr Grossman with a hint of humor. She smiled at this remark.

"Does it fit well?" he asked.

"Oh yes, very well," answered Alison as the hole tightened again around the base after its initial stretch. The strange and pleasurable sensation that followed beyond the first stab of pain of anything pushed into her bottom, was always a little joy. After a pause to feel its presence, she withdrew it and placed it along side the other two on the plastic sheet.

"This one is best for your partners," he said, selecting a headed one of medium size. Unless you have a specific situation in mind, this size is usually universally acceptable in both positions, both openings," he clarified. "As it will be the active device, it is best if it is not too large, as men especially become... frightened." A smile broke on his face for the first time as he made his doubtless often repeated joke. He now picked up both a well worn pad and an even more worn tape measure, together with a felt pen.

"Stand up very straight if you will, and part your legs well. Lift your arms out from your sides and please keep very still so that my measurements will be exact."

Standing as she was instructed, the act of measurement was a further stimulating experience; the touching, the examination, its discipline. She could, embarrassingly, feel her juices trickling down her inside thigh, for her cunt had not closed, and she could smell her body even over that of the leather. Sweat, her musk and leather made a rare combination, she thought.

He was making little marks on her body with the felt pen and running the tape across her skin. He missed nowhere. Even her aroused nipples were marked and measured, the exact curve of her breast, the distension of her buttocks, down between, pulling them hard open to find her anus and on again, pausing at her clitoris, then to her vagina; marked for measurement in both cases by inserting his finger a little way. When he was finished, he told her in a matter-of-fact way that she could get dressed. Alison was exhausted. She had been held at a pitch of extreme excitement for quite some time and now felt as though she had been taken – but cruelly denied – orgasm.

The selection of the harness style was undertaken from illustrations in a well-thumbed and dog-eared book. The different styles had been modeled by a blonde, attractively figured young woman, but indifferently photographed to create that slightly tacky feel to the images that historical pornography has. Alison selected, with considerable and forceful advice, a harness that started with her head, which was to be encased in a 'box' of leather straps. Provision was made for a gag to be incorporated if desired. A tight and high leather collar would encase her neck and then the straps would encircle her breasts, leaving the ends exposed. Dramatic and attractive straps would fan out and down her body, first to strictly retain the waist and then to lace across the curve of her womb at the top of her mound. The male dildo would be directly mounted over her clitoris. Also positioned here was to be a special rubber pad with a cluster of little fingers that would press upon her button as she exerted her own force of the thrust. A wide and parting strap would pass between her legs, holding both of her own internal devices. Movable fastenings ensured that these would be given some motion as the male dildo was used.

Alison could not wait to have this wonder in her possession, though it would be some months before she received a small engraved card to advise her that it was now ready for collection. The difference was that the address for collection was quite different and the time was well into the evening.

She arrived at a very select block of Paris apartments and took the caged lift to the third floor. The brass fitted black door was opened by an attractive and smartly dressed woman.

"Alison Kwik?" she enquired, with a thick French accent, and Alison answered that she was. She was ushered into a small reception room of some quality. Herr Grossman stood up to greet her. He now wore a moderately respectable suit.

"Ah my dear young lady, such a pleasure to meet you again. Part of the substantial sum that my clients pay for my work is to provide them with an initial... trial... should, of course they so wish. Always I find that a little guidance is needed in the fitting of the harness and it is important to me at the level of satisfaction at which I desire to work that they feel that all is satisfactory and comfortable. This cannot be achieved without the practical use of the device. Therefore, Madame Visage" – he gestured towards the woman who had opened the door – "helps me in this matter, in return, of course, for a professional fee for her special services."

Alison now looked with interest at the woman. She was perhaps in her middle thirties, with a slim and well-proportioned body. Her high cheek-bones, restrained dress and hair in a tight bun all gave her a look of refinement and quality edged with a touch of the severe.

"Are you happy with this arrangement?" the woman asked Alison. "Oh yes, I am pleased to go along with whatever Herr Grossman has arranged."

"Then please follow me for we must get on," said Madame Visage and opened the door into the next room. The old man and Alison followed.

The room was a softly lit, typical Paris boudoir in the old style, rich warm and private. Alison saw immediately, laid across a divan, the object of the occasion – the red leather harness.

The woman now took charge of the situation.

"Perhaps, Ms Kwik, you would be so good as to undress, place your clothing over there, so that Herr Grossman and I can fit you with his special garment."

As with the first encounter, Alison felt detached and propelled along by the confidence and experience of others to whom this seemed routine. It was exciting, this surrender of choice. Tonight she had worn a dress, stockings and court shoes. While both the old man and the woman watched almost impatiently, she undressed, placing her clothes with care, trying to retain some dignity. The eyes watched her every move and she felt as though she was stripping for some darker moment, like an interrogation. Even when she had removed her little silk top and matching french knickers, she was still faced with the removal of her stockings and suspender belt. This time she was completely nude, without even pop socks. The woman appraised her with a moment's cool detachment and then picked up the harness. It was quite beautiful, complex and most intimidating. The red leather organs that were intended for her looked even bigger than she remembered them to have been.

"We will proceed with the fitting, if you please. Stand, legs well parted and arms out." It was a command. "And I will do the rest," instructed Madame Visage.

Alison complied and Herr Grossman sat down a little way off, no doubt to watch with craftsman's pride the demonstration of his work. The harness detached into two halves and Madame Visage started by fitting the top. Alison was conscious of the closeness of the woman, the touch of her breath and the subtle tone of an expensive perfume. There came the intimate feeling of being encased as the straps were fastened around her head. The neck collar was drawn tight and she felt the way it forced her head to stay erect. The woman worked quickly and with experience, the many little buckles fastened with ease by nimble fingers.

She felt her torso being brought into difficult bondage. Her breasts rose and were divided to point out to the sides. She saw how stiff the nipples had become and how swollen the areolas were. All around her was again the smell of leather mixing with the smell of two women's bodies and scents. The woman now tightened the corset-like structure beneath Alison's breasts.

"Breath out and hold yourself well in please," requested Madame Visage.

Alison complied and she felt the woman swiftly tighten the straps across her back so that now her waist was drastically pulled in. Madame now reached for a tube of lubricant and methodically coated each of the organs destined for her body.

"This will not be comfortable at first, so just relax. There will be pain as you are penetrated, but it will pass."

Alison did her best to ready herself for the entry of the large dildo. When it came there was no kindness in the forced entry used by Madame, but Alison knew that she would have enjoyed doing the same had the roles been reversed. Even so, a little cry, which must have given some satisfaction to the woman, passed Alison's lips. It was skilfully worked in until Alison felt as though she would split open with the filling force through her cervix and into her womb. The one forced into her behind was nothing like as bad, and it slipped in to immediately give her some rewarding pleasure.

Her crutch and labia were forced wide open by both the device and the width of the harness. So that she would have to walk with parted legs.

While the woman fastened and pulled up the lower section to the that of the torso harness, Alison was able to look down and see the large red dildo for the first time, erect and quivering in front of her, curving up from the base of her mound like men she had so often seen. She was also aware that, at every tremor of the long organ in front of her, the rubber fingers at its base stirred her clitoris in a strange and stimulating way.

The woman now directed Alison's attention to a full-length ornate mirror against the wall. What she saw reflected was a remarkable and totally erotic sight that fired her in a manner she had never experienced before. The muscles of her vagina were in spasm, they started to work involuntarily on the distending solid leather within it and her sphincter, in response, tightened and gripped its plug. The effects of the two dildos became one through the thin membrane wall that separated them. As she looked at herself, she became uncontrollably aroused. With difficulty, due to the severe restriction, she turned sideways and saw pointed breasts and the penis in front with the divided orbits of her buttocks behind capping her long thighs. Her head was encased and warrior-like; indeed the totality was wickedly warlike. She felt an unique sensation of being both dominant and submissive.

Without further ceremony, Madame Visage, in the same flat tone, invited Alison to try the harness. Alison though was uncertain as to what was meant by this offer. Madame then applied lubricant to the dildo, and as if by way of explanation, as though she had done it a hundred times before (and perhaps she had), Madame Visage bent herself over the raised end of the divan. She reached backward and in one practiced movement swept up the length of her dress and tucked it beneath her. Above her black seamed stockings, Alison could clearly see that Madame Visage wore no knickers. The stockinged legs, now parted invitingly, were surmounted by a beautiful full white arse of firm, desirable flesh. The splayed legs ended in expensive, black, long-heeled shoes. Alison was taken aback by this confident display, for it was totally unexpected. Herr Grossman watched attentively from his seat.

"Do not hold back; please go ahead and try your new toy Ms Kwik," came the voice of Madame Visage. "Either hole is permissible... whichever... is your fancy or even both. It is very much part of the service that is offered."

Alison moved forward, feeling the difficulty of walking, the leather stiff and binding, the hips working on the devices within her; all the time feeling the orgasm-generating rub on her button. In fact she wanted so very much to come. The dildo in front of her gleamed with the lubricant already rubbed on it, catching the light.

She moved to between the parted legs so that she was over the raised and offered bottom. She could see the puckered arsehole clearly and in the darker place at the top of Madame's thighs, she could see the hairy and glistening wet rear of the vulva. Frightened but determined, Alison gripped the dildo in one hand and supported her weight on the divan with the other. She entered its round head into the soft lips that were presented. Then, remembering how the dildo had been forced into her own place, she suddenly thrust into the woman with all her force. She was successful in extracting a groan as the back arched in response. With each successive thrust, she gained even more depth. She now held the woman's hips with her hands and moved her own with all her force. Though she was fucking, she was also being fucked and buggered. Such a wealth of sexual sensations promoted the impossibility of restraining the mounting orgasm that was fed and driven by so many exquisite methods of stimulation in her own body. When it came, it wracked her and she gasped and cried out, panting for gasps of air. Her juices squirted from around the phallus within her, soaking the leather between her legs.

She reluctantly withdrew and released the woman. She stood

trembling and instantly wondering what it would be like to use on a man, into his only tight hole, fucking him, gripping his balls so he could not escape the leather prick? The expression on her flushed face was all the real thanks that Herr Grossman needed.

This work was so much more rewarding in his old age than the use of his supreme talents on the horses in old Vienna. The smell which seemed to fill the room, that of this sexual young woman, her sweat, locked with the smell which he clearly knew was the animal perfume of two sated cunts; blended so eloquently with that of the leather he loved to work.

He was content. Madame now reached round and with both hands parted the cheeks of her bottom. It was a signal that she knew Alison would be unable to resist.

IV THE INDELICATE ARRANGEMENT

THE SOCIAL PRESSURES AND DIFFICULTIES of the mid 19th century are sometimes hard for us to understand in our modern times. Yet without money and status, the world of those days was a very terrifying place. This fear was therefore so easily and so often exploited. Lady Beatrice, widowed mother of two young children, awaited the arrival of her close friend Elizabeth. She sat in wealthy splendour in the great morning room of her house. Out through the French doors she could see the gardeners tending the roses that edged the drive. She fidgeted, impatient for her friend's arrival. Her tea was now cold yet she did not wish to ring for more until Elizabeth was with her...

At last the distinctive sound of a carriage's iron wheels on gravel marked the arrival. In the distance she could hear the sounds of pleasantries being exchanged with her butler. The door to the morning room opened and Vickers showed in a smartly dressed young woman, all smiles and warm greetings. Beatrice rose and embraced her friend. She quickly indicated to the tray and the need for its refreshment. Vickers picked it up with care and left them alone.

The irrelevant chatter of two friends passed between them for a while, disturbed only by the arrival of the new tray with tea and small fancy cakes. Only when the door was shut and the servant gone, when her friend and herself each had their fresh cup of fine Indian tea; then did Beatrice, by a change of demeanour, signal that there was more to their meeting that social gossip.

Beatrice looked into her friend's face for a long time, as though searching for the words to begin.

"There is more to your visit today than just our pleasant meeting. I have a dark secret to tell, to unburden from my very soul."

She could see her friend about to interject and raised a hand to stop this.

"No my love, do let me go on, for it is so difficult for me to even find the words to explain, for the thought of this grips at my throat. Even now I do not know quite why I am revealing all this to you for it tears at me to speak of such matters that hold for me nothing but embarrassment and degradation. Though perhaps, my dear friend, it is because of my trust in you and my burning desire for at least one other to know that I feel I must burden you with my secret? I also know that in the past we have had no secrets from each other and that with you of all people I can be both frank and, as this requires it, explicit. I can use words and descriptions that seldom dare pass the lips of persons of our rank and position. You and I have always shared our bedroom experiences with great candour but even you will I know be severely shocked, your senses much disturbed by what I will tell you."

Beatrice certainly had now the full attention of her friend who sat there looking both astonished and perplexed but equally trying to put her companion at ease enouth to tell her this dreadful thing. Elisabeth already thought, her mind running ahead, that they must be about to discuss the matter of some over-amorous lover; what else could warrant such a cautious preamble?

"As you are aware." Beatrice continued. "It is now some eighteen months since the sad death of my beloved John at the age of 26. I am left, with two small dear children. Some would say, that my title, wealth and property were considerable compensations to my loss. I have also had the support of magnificent friends especially yourself to ease my emotional burden. However there are things to which even you were not privy."

Lady Beatrice paused to take a long breath.

"Shortly after the funeral, I was visited by both Mr. Bumstone our family solicitor and John's uncle, Lord Edmond Manning. You may remember him as that rather handsome man with the small black beard at the funeral. At the meeting, Edmund was quiet and Mr. Bumstone did the talking. It would seem, as was slowly and to my dawning horror, explained, that John had never taken the trouble to alter the original family will under which he had inherited both his title and his wealth. Upon his early death, due to this single, negligent fact, I was at a stroke left with absolutely nothing. Truly nothing, nothing indeed except my title and the children. This house, my income, everything, all gone and gone in turn to his uncle, Lord Manning. At the end of that shattering piece of information his irksome task done, Mr. Bumstone left, leaving me now in the hands of the new owner of this very house.

"Lord Manning was cold and most formal, describing my position as a 'pretty pickle'. My hopes rose, as he continued to explain that he already had considerable wealth and a fine house and estate. Then my hopes fell again as he equally explained that however he had to be business like, harsh as such decisions may seem. The situation that I was in was not of his choice nor of his making but rather the fault of my late husband who should have taken the caring and thoughtful time to make provision for his wife and children. He did though, he explained, have some moral responsibility, as I had no close family, to be of help to me. If only for the sake of his late nephew's children.

"Again my hopes rose, only to be dashed once more by his callous cruelty. For he quickly continued saying, as I had come with nothing to this marriage, why should I deserve to have more than the very basics of survival. Therefore he would only fund a small meagre terraced house from some property he owned in a rundown district of London. There would be of course no money for any servants, instead, just enough every year to put food upon the table. Even this was more than most would expect him to do and he felt that he was being quite generous under the circumstances. I would not starve, I would not be homeless, it was adequate; though he, with his cruelty, suggested that I should drop my title or my neighbours would make me a laughing stock. That last statement such a vicious twist of his knife.

"I wanted desperately to break down and cry but instead I met his gaze with all the pride I could muster. Even as the dreadful outcome had been thrown down before me, he paused and with precision of conversation did suggest that there was an alternative. I was already wary of his give with one hand and take with the other tactics and therefore did not show any acknowledgement of hope to provide his satisfaction. He explained, that he would lay this other offer before me, if I was interested? After a significant pause, I said that I was, of course.

Lord Manning then explained, as though selling a horse, that he was a man of peculiar tastes, peculiar sexual tastes. As you will understand he explained, almost apologetically, that such a conversation is most difficult, especially between virtual strangers and this he said he was most conscious of but as I was a married woman, he hoped that he could be exceptionally frank. He could, he said, not explain the exact nature of his alternative unless all propriety was done away with and our conversation be shocking in its nature. The alternative though, in principle, would mean that I would keep the house and the income as long as I and the children would wish it and that he would even enshrine that in a legal paper for my security. Did I therefore wish him to go on was his next blunt question. Again I confirmed that I would hear him out and added with resolution, that it would take a great deal to shock me.

"What he then told me was described as one would describe the terms of some impersonal contract. He rose from his chair and slowly paced the room while I remained seated. I was, his Lordship observed, a most attractive and physically beautiful woman. His late Nephew had shown the most acute taste in marrying me and he felt sure, that I had proved most interesting and lustful in the conjugal bedroom. Even the birth of my two children had not disturbed my slim and perfect figure. Further, my sensitive poise and delicate, even submissive disposition, heightened my attractiveness to him. The fact that I was a titled lady of grace and social position was the final accolade of value. He had up to now enjoyed his special and deviant tastes with young working girls who he bought for money. What apparently spoilt the experiences for him was that for them it was little or no sacrifice to indulge him. To them it was nothing more or worse than the normal hardships of their wretched lives. The handsome prices he paid made their experiences trivial compared to the rewards. So such arrangements never truly satisfied or fulfilled his desires, merely placated them.

"You can understand, my dear Elizabeth, that my mind, though horrified, was also intrigued. I needed to hear more and so, at a wave of my hand and a nod of my head, the description of the alternative continued.

"What would really be valued by him would be an experience that was won only with the greatest of difficulty, given with overwhelming reluctance, even abhorrence, from one who would normally never begin to countenance such sexual indulgences. Someone in fact like myself. He could also extend and expand his tastes as the relationship would be ongoing: something he failed to accomplish with his paid girls. That would give an opportunity to his imagination to be given full rein for the first time and as a connoisseur of such deviant needs he would value that aspect greatly. When you hear what I require, he explained, even you will weigh your position here, the success of your children and the alternative of poor squalor for you and them as perhaps too high a price to pay. To win such an agreement from you would be fair compensation for the loss of property and money which, as I have said, I already have in plenty.

"Dear Elizabeth, what I now surmised was that I was being offered my comfort and security and that of my dear little ones in return for permitting him his sexual attentions. That in the end transpired to be correct in part and would have been little more than many women pay for their pleasant world's provided by men but it was to be far worse than just to partner him in a bed, as I soon discovered as the nature of the terms unfolded. Consider my dismay, having drawn this acceptable by erroneous and premature conclusion, for I had felt, even so quickly, become resigned to the odious role of being his mistress. He was, after all, quite handsome and still young, it would be a price I could pay with out too much difficulty, to lie back and accept his body, especially when faced with the alternatives which were grim.

"Then, Elizabeth, came the small print, as a lawyer might say. I was disturbed, though that is a word that fails dismally to truly describe my reactions inside, not only by the content but by the shocking exactness of the detail. Only the darkest of minds could conceive things with such need for precision. I was amazed that such practices existed or were even contemplated by men. Somehow he knew the layout of the house, perhaps he had been shown this by John on his one visit before we were even wed and stored away such a detail. I have, as you may know, an unused room that leads off from my private boudoir. This would be altered by him. He would send his own workmen to do his bidding. They would decorate this room to his requirements and install a certain piece of special equipment. The room then would remain locked to all, only he having the key. Surely a plan so formed in detail would have been contemplated since the moment of death of my sweet John?

"The arrangement would be thus for (horror of horrors) he continued with layer upon layer of the vilest contemplations. They were, and are of such depravity that I hesitate even now to describe them to you, least you may run screaming from this house"

At this pause, the transfixed Elizabeth leant forward and reassuringly patted the knee of her beloved friend.

"Be strong my love and do not be afraid that I will censure you. It is a dreadful tale you explain and I am aghast that it shoud be true rather than some titillating fiction. If only that were so. If you have had to bear this, the least I can do in the name of our loving friendship is to hear it all, every detail, the more to offer my total support and understanding."

Beatrice drew a breath and showed tears within her soft eyes at this gesture of true kindness.

"It gets so much worse, but as you say, you must hear it, every lurid detail."

She then continued the description of the terms.

"He would need to, dear Elizabeth, visit me at a set time each month to receive his payment in kind, that was how he put it, exactly his words. Prior, even to that first visit, I would be required to undergo a small operation, so minor that it would not tax me greatly (he so caringly reassured me). He would send a surgeon who, due to gambling debts or some such thing, was in his power. This man, upon his instruction, would with his skill remove the hood skin that surrounded the small love button that graced my private parts. He asked if I was aware of the existence of this tiny organ and its effect upon me if it was stimulated. I blushed, yet was forced to concede that I did. He explained that such a removal was common amongst Eastern peoples and not unknown in our country. The surgeon would administer locally some paste of cocaine which would dull any pain and the wound would heal quickly in a matter of days. However, this had to be done (he emphasised this as he said it, raising his voice for the first time), for it was a vital part of his stipulations and beyond any negotiation.

On he then went, fired now almost with the excitement or stimulation of his descriptions as though they were at last released from some dark constraint or secrecy. Such a change would always bear testimony to his control over my body and a feature in a woman that was most stimulating to her and quite beautiful and tempting to his eye.

To support this revelation of my most secret attraction, he would require me to undertake the removal of all the hair from my intimate parts (as is often done in many brothels, he explained), so that I would be wantonly exposed, to his essential examinations. To say that I was horrified, as these requirements unfolded would be an understatement. I sat transfixed as a rabbit lamped by a keeper. All the time he paced the room, explaining each new dreadful requirement (for there were others) in clear, even bold tones, as though he were at his tailor's. The list went on, but I will mention but a few to clarify their direction.

"He would require my punishment, as applied to a harlot in a house of correction. For I must pay with the punishment of my body both for permitting his degradations and for the gift of my wealthy life style, as though I was guilty of the first and greedy for the second. Nothing is without painful cost, he stated with ill-concealed venom.

"He now advised me that he would be employing, at his own cost, for my personal attention, a lady's maid of his acquaintance. He reassured me that she was an intelligent, pleasant and comely girl who would look after my private needs and wardrobe most efficiently and even provide some company. She was, he explained, well-known to him and he to her. She would, with total discretion, assist him in his pleasures with me and look after such tasks as the shaving of my sexual hair, cleaning the room and so on, for she would also have a key, it seemed.

"Lord Edmund now came to the matter of the equipment he would have installed. This was to hold me by its contrivance and design in various positions so making my punishment and his attentions easy, being prepared and strapped to it by his accomplice – this lady's maid. What was most bizarre, my dear Elizabeth, was the description of his main proclivity. I was to be 'rationed' as he put it. It pleased his senses no end apparently for him to always limit the extent of his indulgences. I was to be like a very special dish, created by a fine cook, different and varied by the month. He told me he had found that over indulgence of the senses dulled the appetite. As I was such a rare and special dish, he wished our arrangement never to bore or to sate him. He gave an example. On say one visit, I would be mounted naked upon his device so that my bottom was displayed. This he would first take with his manhood in both my sex and my fundament. He further explained that he would always spend his seed in the latter place so as to avoid my becoming with child. Luckily I have experience of this method as John often used me thus for the very same reason. So those things I could cope with and, as I have said, I expected to have my body thus used. However, he would then beat me with a cane on my behind, for a total of twelve strokes. The girl would attend to me afterwards and it seems, as he kept reassuring me, I would soon mend to be ready again the following month pure skinned and unblemished. It pleases me to mark the purity of a woman's skin but never excessively, he added as though to calm my fears.

" He explained another possibility, warming to the exuberance of his fertile but vile imagination. At perhaps another visit, I would be instead reversed upon this frame of his; strapped in position to expose me lewdly, such was his precise description. He would again take me, though this time spending over my body, even my face. That would be followed by him strapping me with a leather taws to my private place, again twelve strokes. The final punishment and indignity – for there was yet more to come – and something that I must subscribe to on all the occasions of his visits, was to have my bosom bound most tightly with a thin silk cord and at the end, kneel before him and take six strokes of his leather strap upon each of my bound breasts. That, my dear sweet friend, was the wicked and fanciful price to be exacted for my retention of all that I have here.

"Legally it must be an endless contract that either he would terminate and leave me be with all I have or that I could terminate at any time yet revert instantly to my subsistence living. A lawyer would draw a document that would describe all as he had laid it before me, leaving much in an open form to cater for his changing whims and in that lawyer's presence we would both sign it. The shame of that moment alone daunted me for the lawyer would know the dreadful details I was agreeing to. I am sure though that the thought of that additional display of humiliating submission by me pleased his mind no end, for he smiled for the first time when he told me that. He gave me thirty days to think upon the offer, at the end of that time I must either accept or pack my bags and leave. At that he abruptly took his leave of me and his carriage bore him away without another word passing.

"At first Elizabeth, I thought of it as nothing more than the worst of blackmail. I was angry beyond words. The contemplation of this catalogue even eclipsed my grief for the loss of dear John. I am not naive enough to know that there are many strange depravities that some men seek with poor wretched women. Though I must admit that his litany of such sexual evil rocked my very foundations of belief. I think it was the distortion of my body by the surgeon that terrified me most, not for its possible pain or discomfort but that it was such a display of power over another in a disreputable but subtle way. To an end that my hidden and private place where only my own fingers play on occasion (as I know yours play too) or a place only for a lover's intimacy, would be changed by the command of this man forever.

"Poverty seemed the honourable option, at least I would have my dignity and I would foil his perverted desires. Though when I looked around at the house and the grounds and saw my children so happy and content with their nanny and their lovely toys, I trembled at the thought of that changing. Moreover, in time they would need tutors and in the end a start in their adult lives to find a worthy place in society smoothed by the comfort and security that only real money can buy. I was acutely aware that this devil had me, had broken me, knowing in advance that I would never be able to accept his degrading option. If it was but myself I could walk away but could I be so selfish as to condemn my children to be urchins of the streets in ragged clothes? I could not. This man was cunning, the options skilfully measured, just acceptable, just possible to tolerate, for the alternatives were so much worse.

"So Elizabeth, I penned a letter to him to agree his terms. The first ignominy was the lawyer, who was as cold and detached as Lord Manning, as he read out in an emotionless voice every debasement of my body, I felt my pride as a woman die inside me. I scratched my signature as though it had been in my blood. All Lord Manning said after he had signed and after I was in receipt of my copy of this monstrous document, was that he would send the girl, the surgeon and his builders all to commence their work without further delay."

Two emotions held Elizabeth. The first her revulsion at the description of such practices, the second, trying so very hard, from her safe and happy position, to visualise how she would have reacted to such a nightmare had it been her. Strangely, some aspects of her friend's story had stirred her uncomfortably between her own legs to a point where she feared she was a trifle wet. For, if taken as a female fantasy, it had a powerful value. Indeed, later, Elizabeth lay upon the couch in her own boudoir and let her fingers and her contemplation of being in the power of a man, bring her to a climax. At this moment though, there was also the dawning realisation, that Beatrice, her true friend, Mistress of all she surveyed, not only had agreed and signed her name to this regime but after so long a period must have been playing its victim, as so clearly and vividly described. She looked upon her hostess with renewed interest as this fact dawned upon her.

As if to anticipate her friend's direction of thinking or because she had detected a change in the woman's expression, Beatrice broke the moment's silence.

"Elizabeth, I am deeply aware of the thoughts that must now be with you. Yes my dear friend, the surgeon came and with surprising kindness, tact and skill, divested me of my little hood. Yes I daily bear, even this very day, the enhanced sensitivity of that part against my undergarments as it is now so strangely and perversely altered. When I stand before a mirror without my clothes to study this small change, I marvel at the ingenuity of his mind or that of others. In a way that I fear he had not intended it, I feel rather proud of this quite endearing alteration. Equally, naked, displayed and bound I now accept the taking of his member and his abuse, gaining an erotic pleasure to which I am ashamed to admit. He knows that only too well and it heightens his own enjoyment, especially when he examines my button and works it with his fingers.

"It is even possible, though I would never have believed it before, to find the harsh pain of his punishments, especially his cruel strap to my tender sex and aching breasts arousing in a confusing way – at least after the event – for the heat and burning stimulate so remarkably. Again he is aware of that and often makes me describe the sensations to him in detail while the maid looks on.

"Actually the girl he sent, is efficient as his tool and yet kind and comforting in her care of me. So Elizabeth, it has now become but a difficult but bearable price from which I shamefully am learning to take perverted pleasure. Lord Edmond seems satisfied with his bargain and is always enthusiastic in its application which to me – as a competitive woman – I take as a compliment, even trying now to see that I please him with my actions. I am, of course, corrupted and degraded by the unholy alliance. Even so I hope, though I fear it is a forlorn one, that one day he will tire of my body.

He comes tomorrow and it is the month when my body is arched and parted and I endure his strap."

Lady Beatrice turned away from her friend and sobbed for a moment. Then resolve and their joint breeding ascended, and it was suddenly, without a word of further discussion, as though the story had never been told.

"Ah well." She said, a knowing smile passing across her face. "Tomorrow is another day my dear Elizabeth... you must be parched, how neglectful of me, I will ring for Vickers, I'm sure we could both do with more tea, will it be Indian or China?"

V THE STORY OF JOSIANNE

It is best to lay a little background to this interesting tale. It is thought that this story, about this most attractive young woman, was the work of fiction by the notorious Frederick Hanky in Supplices de Josianne. *More detailed research has suggested that he may well have drawn his fictitious account from a real occasion. A first person account about a young woman in her early twenties, does exist in French archives. It seems that it was laid to paper in her later life. She was convicted of the passionate murder of her much older husband for his cruelty towards her while they lived in French Algeria. The court was lenient and spared her the guillotine but sentenced her to ten years imprisonment with the stipulation that she should receive corporal punishment every month of her sentence. The Governor of the prison to which she was sent was one Captain Henri; he had already established a considerable reputation for sexual sadism towards women. It was rumoured that he had been known to indulge in the private pastime of whipping girls most cruelly with a long leather thong.*

Apparently, upon Josianne's arrival at his prison Captain Henri was immediately enamoured with her stunning good looks. He therefore kept her in a special cell away from the disgusting conditions of the prison proper ensuring that she had both a healthy diet and plenty of exercise in the fresh air to maintain her good health and physical beauty. At the end of her first month he established a routine that was to continue for a number of years, up until he was replaced in the post of governor, for Captain

Henri, of course, adhered with enthusiasm to the terms of her imprisonment.

Women who were considered by the prison doctor to be fit for punishment were subjected to a particular method of corporal punishment.

The preferred implement was a 'bull's pizzle' This form of whip had a long history as the device of choice when beating women in both central Europe and north Africa.

The French call it *nerf de boeuf.* The production of an instrument of flagellation, with all the creative effort that goes into the devising of such devices – the sole purpose of which is to inflict pain – warrants some description. It is, as you might guess, skilfully made from the penis of a bull. The hard root of the penis forms the handle, usually with a binding of cord or leather to ensure a good grip. 'Root' is a good name as it resembles the tap root of some large plant, being round and hard, with a dense bundle of fibres within. This root runs on to form the length of the animal's phallus; the centre is removed leaving an outer, tapering, skin. This, if taken when fresh and wound into a tightly tapering spiral, then naturally binds together to form a whip-like form of between eighteen inches and two or so feet. The whole is then treated and cured as with any leather. To produce the cruel and agonising qualities that make the pizzle unique as instruments, it is now soaked for a lengthy time in a leather softening oil such as neat's foot. This oil saturates the fibres and adds substantial weight combined with a rubber-like flexibility.

To the eye, compared with many whips, it seems almost innocent, even innocuous, for the comparatively short length holds no great visual terror. This is but a subtle deception. Its narrow, pale form belies its considerable weight and extraordinary flexibility.

It is this weight, applied to such a small area of contact, encouraged by its desire to wrap instantly to the curving form of female flesh, that promotes a rare fire of agony and damage to the contacted skin, coupled with a transmission of the arm's full force deep into the inner nerves and muscles. With a powerful, trained arm to wield and apply, the flesh will be raised and broken at every stroke. Hence its historic choice in institutions of correction and discipline.

The women's section of the prison where Josianne was incarcerated also held another uniquely female device. Almost universally in Europe and the middle-east, women have been beaten upon some kind of long bench. These benches come in many forms. Most common, is the simple wooden form with wooden or iron brackets to lock the ankles and to lock across the shoulders, leaving the body free to move, as it is said, 'under punishment'. Some have an additional leather strap to hold down the body at the small of the back. Others favour stretching the body painfully tight by fixing the feet and pulling the wrists hard with a rope up to a ring. The Arabs, and the Turks especially, who like to beat women upon the soles of the feet (*bastinado*), often have a form of stocks that hold the legs, bent at the knee, up from the bench, to position the feet at right angles to the floor and so ideally positioned for the cane or pizzle.

However, both the Germans and the French have used a far more unpleasant form of bench. This design is known as the 'raven'. It is still a low bench set upon four strong legs, but it is only boarded to about half its length and this board is usually covered in blunt iron spikes. The other half is just a square rail, turned to be a triangle in section with an upward edge. At the end of this are a pair of iron manacles. Its use is as follows: the poor, naked, victim first crouches down astride the rail. She either for herself, or by the hands of the torturers, opens the labia of her sex before placing her crutch upon the rail. Instantly, they will grab up her ankles, bending her knees so she is like a jockey, and lock them into the manacles. This presents the soles of her bare feet and also forces her forward to take her weight upon her pubic bone and clitoris. Her wrists are held at the sides of the front of the bench either by manacles or straps. While she has strength her arms try to support her torso to keep her breasts from pressing down upon the painful studs, inches beneath them.

So positioned upon the raven, a woman's buttocks, thighs and the soles of her feet are available for corporal punishment. When her body inevitably convulses and moves as the strokes are applied, her most tender and intimate area works upon the rail and the uncontrolled arching of her back drives her breasts, time and time again upon the blunt studs bruising them. It is said that such a bench was called the 'raven' for it pecked mercilessly at the body.

It was such a raven that this prison had, though *sans* the pointed studs, for they had another chosen refinement.

We now offer an extract from translated account that M. Josianne has left.

✻ ✻ ✻

It is now some time since my arrival at this prison. Today, is yet again that day I dread so much, for it is the day before that time allotted to my sentenced punishment. For others, it would be still be a day away but for me my ordeal starts upon this very night. On one hand I must have some thanks to offer up; that I enjoy adequate accommodation in this desolate place. I have books to read and improve my mind and education. That I also daily enjoy good victuals and pleasant exercise in the sun in a small walled garden. I have besides, the companionship of an aged soul, an inmate like myself but trusted to look after me and give me conversation. I know also something of the dreadful state that others endure, the cramped dark cells, the stench, and the rotten food. Upon my arrival the good Captain Henri made sure I was aware of my privileges through a personally conducted tour. Yes, in these things I am lucky for I could easily perish from disease alone as others often do.

I have eaten little, for my appetite leaves me when I consider the impending ordeal. Amar has washed me in the tin bath and used the perfumed soap that he supplies. Before the wash, I always spread myself naked, legs parted, at the end of my divan. Amar then soaps me there and with her kind skill, shaves away the stubble that has grown. I must be bare there, hairless like an Arab woman, for he has taken that taste from his time in this country. While I am naked I check my body again in the mirror I have been given, it is my woman's' luxury. My dark hair is rich and long and my face is young and healthy, skin darkened by the sun. It is a cheeky face that looks back at me, full lips that I will soon make up with rouge. My bosom pleases me, now ripe and recovered, as always, still firm, the ends turned up, crowned by rich dark nipples that look so naughty when I move slightly to one side. My slim waist and below a curving belly a bold, shaven mound, all please me as I turn before the mirror. I rotate to inspect my round bottom and the backs of my long thighs. Thin white lines crisscross the otherwise perfect skin. Amar tells me that after many years of punishment I will be changed in these areas for ever. Already, I notice that I bleed less and the bruises heal more quickly; it is as though my body is learning ways to outwit their tortures as the months pass. Although I cannot yet escape the dreadful pains, for they know their job too well, even so to understand that I survive the agony and that it always passes, helps. Even so, I will lie upon my stomach for a few days afterwards, know nights of discomfort and see my pretty feet so swollen that I can only walk with care. Amar is most kind and caring and at these moments she tends me like a child, washes the wheals oh so gently, applies sweet balm and ointments that aid healing and prevent infection where they are broken and above all wipes my tears and sings me ancient nursery songs in her language that I do not know but am comforted by.

Later as the sun sets swiftly into the night, the oil lamps are lit and after my lengthy make up it is time for Amar to lace me into my corset so that breathing is difficult and my waist impossibly small. I then roll on each decadent fishnet stocking, attaching the suspenders and placing the black patent shoes upon my feet. Over this I don a simple cotton cloak and Amar unlocks my door to escort me to his rooms.

We pass through iron gates, opened by leering, slovenly guards and we enter the private world of Captain Henri, Master of this accursed place. His accommodation is sensibly sited far from the night cries of the prison's inmates. When I am before his door I am empty inside, assailed by that gnawing that comes as my stomach cramps with anticipation. Amar knocks and then opens the door. I enter and it closes behind me.

Everything is always the same. I come monthly like some rationed treat, his caged pet. At first it was all so new, but now that I know what to expect it is far worse. My imagination makes it worse, knowing so much makes it worse. It is all there, the yellow glow of lamps, the smell of perfume and spices, the quality furniture from Paris. Then there is the large table set with food and wine and of course near by, the small table of rich veneered wood, laid out with the nasty things with which he will inevitably hurt me.

He is there and such a handsome man to be a sadist, why couldn't he have been vile and ugly? What is it about me that obsesses him, that is my unanswered and constant question? He is smoking a long Russian cigarette, and I catch its rich aroma. We never talk. Beneath his silk dressing gown he will be, as always, naked. A beautiful, classically male, body. He nods to acknowledge my arrival and draws deeply upon the cigarette. He nods again and I know to slip off my cloak. I stand there being minutely observed as he takes a sip of dark wine. A hand beckons me to approach him and I walk slowly across the deep pile of the Turkish carpet. I am now very close and the smoke swirls round me, I dare not look at his cruel eyes. The hand waves sideways and I slowly part my legs, further and further at each instruction from the hand. They are, as he desires, now set embarrassingly wide apart. The instructing hand signals for me to arch. My hands clasp together behind me and I thrust out my shaven sex towards him, curving my body as much as I can, in the seductive motion of an eastern dancer.

He puts down his wine and cigarette and leans forward. He extends his manicured hand and inserts first one, then two, then three fingers into me. They stretch me, they explore and I of course find it pleasurable. He moves them slowly, methodically, until I start to tremble a little in my tensed, stressed legs. The fingers are finally withdrawn and slipped into his mouth, he is tasting me for I am now very wet – something I cannot help or control.

The hand now makes the rotation signal. I stand up, turn round, part my legs again and bend fully over. I then reach behind me and place my hands upon each of my tightened cheeks and dig in the fingers, I pull the division apart. I have learnt all these routines so that now I respond correctly to the silent signals, as some trained animal might in a circus. Amar has also shaved this area between my cheeks and around the puckered hole. He hates hair upon the body of a woman. He wets his fingers again, dipping them between my labia, then two fingers are forced into my anus, there is the usual, only minor discomfort at first for that place is well used to such attentions, indeed, ones far worse than this.

When he has finished he gets up and rinses his hands at a gilt washstand. I stay bent, cheeks held open, for I never do anything in his presence with a direct instruction.

When he returns he is now naked. He has oiled his erect penis. He stand behind me, holds my hips and with one motion forces it in, right in, deeply in, choosing the small hole of my bottom. I cannot help but cry out and let go of my hold on my cheeks. He has me now and I grip my ankles to steady myself. He likes to take it almost out and then force it back in until his body closes with my rump. My hole is erotically stretched by his thickness and I feel him so far within me, touching my insides. Sadly, I admit to enjoying this usage. My aroused vagina drips upon his carpet and I hate him, hate him more for I am so weak, so easy to pleasure. I hate him and myself for I must climax. Hate him even because he makes me hate myself, despise my primal arousal for I cannot stop myself. He holds me tightly while I shudder and gasp. Then as suddenly as he was upon me, I am abandoned.

I rise slowly shaking and turn to face him. I sink to my knees and confront his sex. It is soon in my mouth and I must perform this vile and degrading task until he thinks it cleaned and pure. My mind cannot think while my tongue works away, I am so disgusted to taste myself and my nausea rises.

He gives me wine to wash my mouth and I eagerly gulp it down.

I stay kneeling, arms now braced together behind my back so that my breasts are thrust out, forced as they are, unnaturally upwards by the top of the corset. The captain pulls his chair closer, in his hand are the special pincers. The empty hand, gently, like a lover, teases the left nipple till it hardens, it feels nice, it thrills me. Then with such considered precision he steadies the areola between finger and thumb and applies the mouth of the pincers. They squeeze, they twist, they extend. I cry. Saliva runs from my rouged mouth. The right one is then so carefully punished in the same way. He looks into my face as it contorts with agony, his is so calm, so sadistically cold.

"Basin" it is his first word.

I get up, my nipples sore – and unnaturally elongated – are burning. I fetch the enamel basin from the stand and I again kneel before him and hold the basin beneath my chin. I tip my head back and open my mouth. The urine is warm, I gag and I swallow as best as I can. It runs down my chin, drips into the basin. He pisses for a long time.

When my head goes down again, some runs between my breasts and down inside my corset.

I am signalled to brace my body again. He knows the delay has allowed my nipples to become more tender; this time the pincers are very cruel and they leave a little blood at the end. I wanted to scream but he would violently slap my face if did, I can only cry and moan, I try not to beg for he likes that and when I am forced to he smiles a rare smile, as though it is a silly but understandable request, as though he would like to comply but with deep regret cannot.

It is all such a strange routine for I know now every step to come, every stage, every moment of intense pain that will induced, so there are no surprises. Sometimes I crave for it be altered. I had learnt the ritual slowly guided by those hard slaps to my face when I made a mistake or when what I did was not to his liking or when I failed to grasp my duties. At those moments in my education, the vice like grip came to the hair at the back of my head and the flat of his hand across first one then the other cheek, my head left reeling.

The next ordeal I always dreaded, thought about afterwards during my long nights. I was upon the divan propped up by fine cushions, my legs pulled up to each side of my chest, held there by my hands, feet by my head, in essence bent double. He laced on a sheath of black leather, methodically and in front of me, leaving only the purple head of his prick showing. The special sheath was studded along its length with blunt metal points. They were, of course, rounded and posed no threat of serious physical damage, that was not their purpose. No, coupled with his length and thick girth, they would abrade me, punish my tight vagina, bruise me so spitefully. Equally the position he favoured for his entry ensured that I would take his full penetration, feel his engorged head deep in my womb, stretching my cervix, hurting me as at the same time I was pleasured, such a cruel twist.

His breath was upon me, his entry agony. His deep thrusts agony. I cried and whimpered to be taken so, to know such pain inside me, yet tomorrow I knew that this pain, real as it was, would seem so trivial. He worked hard for he was at last fully aroused, my suffering face so close to his, I smelt his sweat just as he smells my complete submission to his will.

Naturally, Captain Henri wished to hurt me, wished to degrade me, I obeyed, I complied, I suffered because it would be infinitely worse not to. There was still my fear, my cold dread of these monthly encounters, always four long weeks to wait for the next. Now though, perhaps through experience and time there were no unknowns, and I felt some power. Even as the punishment sheath entered and left me and I endured its every bruising inch I was aware that I had power. This evil man hunched over me, grunting and straining, drinking deep of my suffering, was no longer a detached sadistic force, cold and frightening. He was real and needing the drug he could draw from me, from his addictive fixation. As I suffered my hips involuntarily thrust back uncontrolled as I succumbed to my animal reflexes to his entry. My passage, in some weirdly masochistic way, tightened its muscles and gripped him. I felt power, my female power. I came again with a spasm of tightness on him, my liquids spurting out around his sex. That made me feel dirty. How could I show a reaction of pleasure to his deliberate cruelty? As always, I let him win by this display.

He pulled out of me, stood over me, panting, that dreadful prick in its black cloak, hard, large, glistening with my liquids upon its leather.

He left me knowing that I could not move from my exhaustion. He removed the sheath and washed his genitals. Then, as though nothing had happened, he sat and relaxed, lit another Russian cigarette and drunk deeply of the wine. He watched me for I was opened legged still holding my calves, still bent and exposed, my hole gaping and ravished but not daring to move.

The hand beckoned again and I crawled to him, for I could not walk. He pointed to the little table, I knew what he wished me to collect. The dreadful dildo, long, carved, three inches thick, a polished handle, all so beautifully made by a craftsman. I offered it to him, up on my knees, shaking slightly. When he took it I turned completely about and pressed my head and breasts to the carpet, so better to raise my arse before him. He wet the pointed head at my vulva, then as I screamed he forced it into my fundament, the sudden stretching of this tight hole. Such massive, deep filling of my body drew a sharp, extreme, pain. For this procedure he let me scream, desired that I scream. He left it in buried up to its polished handle, observing from his chair how it held me so open, the ring so tightly stretched that the pain did not subside. When my convulsions eased at last, he pulled it out, I heard it drop to the floor with a dull thud. I knew that my anus would be left open for him to study; it was then that he dropped the glowing cigarette butt into this dark, void. He always did. I twisted and writhed upon the floor before him, demented, just as I always did until at last I could internally extinguish its glowing fire.

He stood over me as I cried and he masturbated, watching my prostrate form coldly, his hand moving back and forth until his face tensed and white viscous liquid was sprayed across my bare flesh. It was his silence that degraded me most: I was not worth his breath.

I took up my cloak and shoes and slowly, with great difficulty, stood up. With awkward steps of pain I crossed the room to the door and left. Amar, oh kind Amar was there, she said nothing but wrapped my cloak around me and with my arm across her old strong shoulders I made the slow journey back to my cell, the pains deep within me reinforced by each step. When I was there, Amar would let me cry myself to sleep. Tomorrow Captain Henri would preside at the ceremonial beating of a number of inmates upon the raven. I would be one, a number to him only. Tomorrow he would again be the Governor, dressed in his immaculate captain's uniform. Ensuring the efficiency of the allotted punishments, ensuring each girl endured the maximum taste of her rightful sentence, full value must be given and taken by the State... always. Tomorrow he was the arm of the court of compassionate Justice that had spared my neck but needed to constantly remind my body of its magnanimity, of its gracious leniency – but also of the cold efficiency of its bureaucracy.

So tomorrow came, as it always did. I was still sore and punished by the previous night. The large stone room of that ancient prison stunk. Stunk of vomit, of urine, of sweat, of fear, the very walls of stone were impregnated by the countless screams. It was a dark place, deep beneath the ground, built of grey blocks, implacable and uncaring constructed so far from the hot sun. The room seemed full of men. Rough, coarse overseeers, the Captain crisp and pressed, aloof and distant from the event, hidden in the shadows. The raven was there, in the centre, in pride of place. It was old and massive. A low construct of blackened timbers, on squat legs, riveted iron brackets holding it to the slab stones as though it might sprout wings and try and escape this hole. The wooden planks were polished to a fine sheen that glowed in the light of the single lamp that hung above to illuminate the arena of suffering. They were polished by history, by a thousand young breasts and sweating bodies that had caressed the wood with their sweet, young twisting forms, now their only lover.

From this ran the evil rail, deeply stained; the very beak of this black bird. The flags beneath, dark, drenched with constant offerings of female blood.

A table, out of the light, held the lead troughs, each with a perfect pizzle drinking quietly of the feeding oil, waiting till they were called to work again.

We were there also, a handful of young women, naked, shaved, chained to the wall, wrists high above our head, stretched up, well onto our toes, bodies taut and straining, facing the wall, our varied backs and bottoms turned to the room. Our breasts touched the stone which hardened our nipples with its cold kiss. I was clean, they were dirty and seldom permitted to wash. I could smell them upon each side of me, hear their panting breaths. One, who was perhaps new, a stranger to this terror, cried quietly and privately.

Voices, called instructions, things must start. The young girl beside me was briskly unchained.

"Number?" said a voice.

Her soft response, chanted it, in a voice used to murmur to a friend upon a white pillow.

"She can be bound." said a voice.

The added refinement. God had graced her with full breasts that could be bound, how lucky she was! Strong hands would pull her arms to her back. Another would dextrously wind the thin, cutting cord, pulling it cruelly tight at every meticulous turn; jerking her body, as Amar jerked mine as she laced my corset. That soft voice again, pleading, gasping as they hurt her bosom so much, as her perfect breasts were transformed into straining, darkening orbs. The deep aching starting, the slowly growing agony of such binding successfully fulfilling its purpose. Then, when her uncontrolled and writhing body drove these hardened breasts so as to press them against and further polish the boards, there would come such a rare pain that would fill her chest. Even beyond a week's passing they would still be tender from this refinement. So as I watched, the process of the binding was soon expertly finished and a little liquid seeped from the dark, stretched nipples as a testimony to the pressure of this procedure.

Barked instructions, hands upon her, taking her to the raven. Forcing her astride then her hips down; skilled fingers pulling at her labia, parting her lips, her wet, opened slot now kissing the beak. The metallic sounds of the manacles closing upon the ankles, then her sounds, her sharp cry as they rocked her body forward on the rail. That edge now against her pubic bone, against her button that should be played with and sucked. I knew of course how much this hurt. Her wrists were locked to the sides of the bench, clawed fingers gripped, desperate to support her, to keep he up, keep her torso weight from her poor breasts.

"At the instruction of the court, the prisoner will receive corporal punishment in the correct fashion. Ten allotted strokes with the approved instrument to the feet, ten to the thighs, ten to the buttocks." The Captain spoke, an authoritive slow pronouncement.

There was a pause, a silence from those present, except for the moans of the girl on the bench, except for the continued crying of the woman upon my wall.

"Commence punishment!" This was barked and reflected back by the walls. The overseeer, now stripped to his waist, select a pizzel, a cloth was carefully wiped along its length till all the oil was removed.

They were always first; the up-turned soles of the feet, delicate small female feet. That, soft innocent place between the pads of the toes and the pad of the heal where the pizzle would first kiss with its fire. A place of a myriad nerves which was why it was so favoured. Feet pressed together by the iron rings that held them. The feet first, because, meticulous, thoughtful minds that somewhere calmly consider such things, knew this to be best, knew it would be the worst pain of all. A pain that invaded the brain, that contorted the muscles of the cunt, that caused a spasm within the sphincter, that constricted the womb, that inevitably released the bladder to gush over the rail. That ran like a bead of fire along the arched spine till it exploded within the head, for this pain was appreciated to its full by a fresh victim, best tasted before other attentions dulled even a fraction of their senses.

We stared at the wall, I and the women with me. I observed, with academic detachment that the pizzel makes a strange noise, like a bird in flight close to your ear. There is then a different sound depending upon the place of contact. The feet one sound, the thighs another, the cheeks of a beautiful female bottom the loudest of all, for here it engaged two tensed orbs of flesh at once, missing nothing, following with its elastic flexibility the curving path of the rounded flesh. You became an expert. You listened to it on others and you listened to it on yourself. You always heard these sounds for they waited until you were almost quiet again, they were patient, they wanted the contorted nerves to fill fully with their burning of an indescribable form of pain, they wanted you to know most clearly and remember precisely each stroke.

A single voice droned, with long pauses in between. " One... two... three." The sequence of five sounds as you faced the wall. The bird in the air, swooping, the bull's prick striking the young flesh, then the dreadful scream; those screams I will always hear, as well as I remember my own. The writhing torso upon the boards hurting its blackened breasts, the gyrating pelvis torturing its own cunt upon the rail; that is four, the voice that at last counted, that is five.

I did not see her carried out. I did see, when unchained and turned to face the raven myself, the drips of her blood upon the floor, wet, catching the light; the blood upon the raven's rail, blood from her dear sex.

I told them my number.

"She can be bound" cried the voice.

I looked away from my breasts, felt the hands, felt the first turn. What was I at this moment to Captain Henri, his eyes revealed nothing as I dared to fix mine upon them. The twine bit into my breast and it became a perfect sphere, no longer up-turned and provocative, he tugged and grunted with the effort, I opened my dry mouth to gasp, letting them bind and hurt, I was so used to this routine.

So I watched, as a distraction, the bare chested overseer. Slowly he stroked the length of the pizzle with his cloth, wiping away the blood. He was a professional, his eye upon my naked form, watching the binding, glancing quickly over the rest of my body, wishing he could rape me. I was another's property. He must be content with the other girls. I could see him appraise me, evaluating my thighs, my naked bottom, making decisions as to where to precisely strike each stroke. We both knew that we would soon know each other more intimately than any penetration could achieve. For he would use another prick upon me and I would move for him uniquely, reveal my tender spots to which he could return again and again. I would find for him a voice that no orgasm could ever stir from my lips. We would be, for a while, inextricably linked. I would bleed for him, like a virgin's cunt, I would spasm in the cheeks of my bottom as though delivering his sired child. I would show him an erotic beauty of movement that few men would ever see. I would never, ever forget him, for he was my true lover, his caresses burned upon me, deep within my private senses.

VI   THE RED ORCHID

There is a thin line between reality and madness. The victim struggles to hold onto the real world while their mind desperately seeks to escape. This conflict has always remained the same since time began and the inhumanities that we so 'justly' perpetrate in the name of state or religion continue unabated. The greatest challenge the victim finds is to anticipate and to please, for when those above you are so feared, their satisfaction with your behaviour becomes a paramount focus for your dysfunctional mind...

Today my world is dark. I see taboos that also spur my desire. Today I look into the glass, the mirror of myself, my knowing, my need to know. My body, which is also me, is ripe and ready. With me, in the picture was my pubescent self, standing beside, still in my woman's world. I must take her with me, share with her my knowing to a time when she only guessed, only gasped with surprise at the wonders that were but a dream.

I have a blade, I let the pure clean steel caress my skin, take away my mark of woman, my covert hiding of my sex and return me to the youth within. The place is now open and running with my wetness. I cut the tangled hair from every, intimate fold and every little hollow, pulling, parting as I work to undress it. This I do for others, as they have told me to. They need it seen without impedance, I must be clearly seen. I say look and with long fingers red varnished tipped I pull it wide to pout its guarding lips.

The dark hooded people have asked me now, today, to drink. I am instructed with slow clarity on how drink. They share their experience, their calculated procedure with me, as though to rehearse a melodrama. Naturally, I will be questioned during the drinking and by nature of the method will not be able to answer and so must travel fully the path they have long practiced. A small iron closes my nostrils, I must therefore either drink or breath but first I always have to drink, and there is always more than I can drink with any comfort. So then the rushing, urgent requirements of my lungs, drive gulp upon gulp to seek and desperately find the precious air that lies beyond the water.

If I could but see myself I would be dramatic, and I'm sure beautiful, to observe. For I am stretched and arched upon an ornate pedestal; I form a curving shape, my wrists and feet pulled strenuously to sustain the tableaux. In their cloaks of anonymity they generate within me a virgin's pregnancy. It seems I am with child. I am slowly swollen and distended and the agonies of childbirth are and will be nothing to compare with this conception of Satan. My waters cannot break, even though within me my bladder yearns for a relief that is denied to me by a subtle plug: no aqueous relief for this invasion.

I am kneaded and prodded as though upon a market stall, and when they decide that I have drunk enough, leather straps corset my form, not to nip my waist, but instead to torment my beating heart and drive me to pleading suffocation.

With probing fingers I am induced to empty myself, the plug removed, I urinate my pain away and touch my place even as the warm and golden flow washes my urgent fingers that tease me to my floods of joy. Then arched back and stretched I am filled again. In my demented suffering I lose count of how many times I show my form in this way and drink of their water.

Today, from beneath their priestly cloaks I am shown, one

upon another, the male rods that torment and delight – such cruel pleasure. But I must kneel, my arms encircled by the cords that mingle with my embracing love. My mouth finds each a new sweet tryst. I both drink of new nectar, and let it drip upon my breasts. It is an exquisite service. They think of my degradation. They know that my pinioned arms will also deny my burning need and I am left moist and unsatisfied.

Today I am to be shown at my best (or so I am advised). There is simplicity in this service. I rotate before a silvered copper mirror, least I am denied my own display. Yes, I agree and see myself as others see me. Yes I agree, it is so very beautiful. I was not aware just how beautiful a young female body could be when displayed this special way. I consider how I also must appear from behind. The taut back, strained muscles, round posterior, down and on to the calves and feet. An expression of my painful tension, a moving sculpture of my stretched sinews. Each muscle that screams my pain within, equally displays to the observer a tortured glory of a woman's perfect form. I am grateful to please their eyes in this eloquent way, for I am but their vision and they are not inside my torment. Time passes with the ponderous slowness of an old clock, they only ask their questions and still no answers come for none I have. I wish that I were a playwright and spin some pretty tale for them but they are a cold and unyielding audience. So weights are added to my slender ankles till the mists of pain steal me away.

Today, they have brought me a facsimile of their male reality but carved with bitter points and unnatural size and girth. It is foolish I know but I protest its size and latent cruelty, aware of its intention I suggest impossibility. They now watch, for I have a choice. I am right, it hurts me, so strange to hurt one's self so much, yet I am compelled, for if it is not by my hand then by one of theirs. They have explained that they would force and hurry. I have taken it now, amazed that it is possible. See how it fills me, distends and opens, an augmentation that tears at my soft tissue. As much as I am parted for their eyes I am expanded within. The aching therefore grows. Again and again, I must take it in both hands and withdraw and then insert it upon their command; always further in, though I have not the strength. I must do this till I shake with my perverse pleasure. Strange is my body and its strings that I pull.

Today they are most certainly not content. My answers are inept. So to offer correction I am to learn another of their endless ways. This also when confronted seems impossible. This is the Devil's way they say and tell me that I am but the Devil's dirty child. So I am tight restrained, folded and compressed – my legs to my breasts till even they are squeezed. This presents my fundament between my parted division. Fire comes from such a depth of ancient knowledge. I am impaled the martyrs way and such arousal and desire comes upon me that I drip my pleasure from my flower. In my submission, I am again to service all their needs. I part black cloaks and find the ridged forms that captivate my senses. They say it is my duty, such action a humility. This time I drink and drink again. The drops are precious and fill me with the tastes of mother sea, such salted swollen forms upon my throat.

Today I am to rest – or so they say. More questions must be written in their tomes. Their clerk meticulously, quill pen ever scratching each implemented action, my sounds, my cries, my tears. I am strapped upon a stool like some small and naughty child. Cords are placed upon my wrists in advance of what is to come. The scribe waits his line complete. Round oranges of iron are brought, storing the fire. So subtly just too warm to hold for long yet so innocuous. One goes beneath each lifted armpit. And quickly the wrist ropes cross my arms and are tied tight behind. As I start to scream and the clerk begins to write again, I wonder in surprise that but warm iron could cause such growing agony and that equally how any person of normal mind could conjure of a torture such as this. I writhe upon my stool, though it is well fixed within the ground. My plump breasts bounce seductively no doubt, with my witless gyrations. I shine, glossed by a copious sweat of suffering. When the globes cool I am questioned again while they are heated afresh. Three times my armpits are warmed so kindly least they suffer chill. I wonder in my distraction how my screams are written down?

Today I return, refreshed and rested. They have such patience and also others to amuse them in my absence but in the end I am not forgotten. Equally I receive no personal attention, not probing questions. Just as many times before, I stand upon my toes, in a dank, dark, stinking place, arms pulled at the elbows till they meet behind and small steel hooks to hold me there by each dear breast that now turn unnaturally upwards by their fastened ends.

Today they are not with me. Instead I find a man upon the cobbled street. I do not see his face. He touches my cunt, lifting my dress. He feels its smoothness, shaved for his fingers touch. Later, I place my long legs over his broad shoulders and accept him inside me. He is warm and it is so new, a beginning. It hurts in a nice way and I still want him much deeper. I know that he has filled me, filled my womb. Later, what he has left appears and trickles down my inner thigh, it is a most pleasing sensation and must therefore be repeated. Such are my simple dreams of love.

Today I yearn for pain. They anticipate this. I lie upon my stomach bound tightly to a board, so very tightly; legs together. I am comforted by the close confinement. Little claws of metal are used to force apart the cheeks of my round bottom. They whip my fundement with a searing leather thong. It is an unique sensation, pain and pleasure unite as I rise to my climax. Still this tender opening is flogged, methodical strokes, unrelenting. It is now just pain. Inevitably, my blood runs down my crack and between my thighs.

Today I must ride the wild horse, it is a horse, such a beautiful horse; a carved horse from my childhood dreams, painted as from a fairground. I ride upon my horse, though it is not for a child, where paint and gilded leaf should mingle with a carver's skill there is only stained oak and iron. Its saddle does not comfort and support over fantasy hedges and endless meadows, why should it, why should it be so kind? This is for a dammed woman to ride and where horsehair and leather should pad only a sharp edge lies. I ride it like a jockey, my ankles high and knees well bent but for stirrups I have manacles. Where my hands should guide the reins only iron bracelets serve to hold me bent forward in my equestrian posture. If observed I am as a jockey, arms low and bottom high, but between my legs I am slowly and inexorably tortured by an ancient method. It is a deliberate position, so cunning and calculated, they are at their most creative. The bone of my pubis and my secret purple joy are exactly set to suffer upon the cruel edge. No leather crop spurs on my mount instead it is my round, taught flanks, so raised and ready that are repeatedly driven on to grind and move upon the beast by stroke upon stroke of well soaked leather. When I am rested from the whip, it is my anus that is opened by the wedges, driven in by well-judged blows. This is a stallion of torment. My juices flow and the perfume of my rich sweat, rises like the steam of a driven animal.

Today, pious men discuss me, in quite, dispassionate voices, I stand before them in my ragged and torn smock. It is still difficult for me to stand and walk. They dispute between themselves about my youth, my health, my strength, my capacity, my performance, my obvious evil. All is duly evaluated and of course recorded. The surgeon comes and makes his speech and most professional of observations. More rest, more salve, more broth, more wine and I will know again with clarity every test to which my sensitivities are subjected. So the good doctor buys me peace for, as I have already explained, they are patient.

Today, it is at last the whip. Oh yes, I have been used already with thong and quirt but for them that is incidental, specific in its nature. I have frustrated them and failed to bend my wicked will, enjoyed and spent my juices. So this is not torture but punishment, they see a difference. The whip is delicious to my strumpet's thoughts and strumpet's flesh. Even its concept its presence in my mind finds me spending to my eager touch upon my hardened button. I wonder at my un-sated lust, my strange desire to please their minds with my endless suffering and yet how I suffer so dreadfully, I am driven to heights of passionate arousal by my drug pain. So I divest myself of my rags and offer my nakedness to their eyes again. I wait, and thus prepared, let its fingers of cruel fire kiss my taut flesh. They have stretched me tight so that I will feel it best, be firm and unyielding least my movement deny even the smallest lessening of the leather's force upon me. They care about these little details of professionalism, the true art of their trade. I am not to know its journey, its little searching visits, I can only speculate and wait, even as the lash whistles through the cold air I must still guess its destination. I am hung head down from a timber beam that spreads my legs as wide as those of a virgin upon her wedding night, as wide open as her eyes. My wrists hold me fast to an iron ring set within the flagged floor and a powerful winch has drawn me as if I was racked. The scribe imparts to his velum in a fine hand each stroke and, like a ship's captain, their port of call. I wait for it to find my tender place so well opened and waiting. They do not disappoint. I am at last raped by the tongues and in hell's true fire, entered by its tips. I scream for them to drown their cold enquires. I scream and bleed for them. They whip me well.

Today is a holiday. To celebrate I am beaten upon the dark ends of my breasts, a well made rod of sappy twigs. I see my own blood drip from my teats like a phantom's milk feeding its satanic young. Their mouths, hidden in the darkness of their cowls, suck my punished ends and I cry like a small child for it hurts so very much. My pubescent self is again with me, we embrace. Sometimes I wish I could return and embrace my innocence yet they know I am still innocent. I masturbate again, today I have masturbated nine times. My orchid is red and gorged.

Today there is no more. The dark figures are not there, nor there earnest clerk, nor their insoluble questions. I am in a cage but do not know if I am a prisoner. I may have incarcerated myself. There is a door that will not open and a window beyond, a small window that is open and a small window that is barred. Should I shrink and with magic try to pass its portal, leave my tight cage? I notice that I am shackled, and quite naked, so painfully. Across the cell, I see my pubescent self, I am also naked and shackled, the distance is small and we can smell each other, we share the same smooth sexes but we can no longer touch. They have parted me from myself. My fingers fail to reach my red orchid, chained and bent double as I am. I can only watch the dew form upon its sweet petals as it opens to welcome the world.

VII ALICE AND HER FRIEND

LICE AND ROSEMARY WERE THE SAME AGE and grew up together in an orphanage. It was 1843, and by the standards of the time, it had been a reasonable place. Privately and philanthropically run, it tried to show some compassion for its inmates. True, their bare bottoms had frequent encounters with Matron's birch twigs, and true they worked at endless and boring tasks while there was light from the stained glass windows. But they had shoes, beds and plain food. They learnt to read and write and above all, the girls learnt to serve, for that was their destiny decreed by the Bible. They studied the Bible on Sundays.

So it was that Alice and Rosemary were groomed for domestic service. So good was their training that the orphanage held a reputation in society as a place to acquire good young staff who would give no trouble and knew their duties. At the age of fourteen, they were both selected for positions in the same house. It was at that moment that they were given the Christian names of Alice and Rosemary. It was of no account what their real names were, their new employer decided, as they stood before her. Alice and Rosemary suited them and it suited the employer.

For these two fourteen-year-olds, it was a strict but reasonable house to work for and they grew both in age and experience as they practiced their skills and duties. They became used to the endless tasks that stretched from early fire-lighting to late evening duties. There was fun though in the kitchen with a happy and generous cook, so they ate well and grew into strong and attractive girls.

They enjoyed their one Sunday a month off, when they could walk in the park and get cheeked by the young men. They had slept together and cuddled together in the orphanage and though they now had separate single cots in the attic of the house, their stirring hormones led them to extend their loving friendship and explore the wonders of each others' bodies, climbing boldly into each others arms at night.

Things changed when this hardworking but comfortable household had to uproot and leave for India where the Colonel had to serve with his Regiment. There was no place for Alice and Rosemary, who were now eighteen. Honest and good though their service had been, they would be out on the street, armed only with a good reference. By chance, the Colonel's wife was asked by an acquaintance what she would do with her staff and so, because of this contact, the two girls made an arduous journey to new employment in the West Country.

They were collected by coach in town. Their hearts fell as the final part of the journey went on and on across increasingly desolate land. A bitter, grim-faced man was at the reins, huddled in his greatcoat. He ignored every question they asked him.

At last they passed through the gates and approached the house up a long, tree-lined drive. An immense park surrounded them. The house was massive and bleak and it loomed out of an evening mist. They entered through the servants' door as darkness fell. A housekeeper, dressed in black with a large bunch of keys hanging from her leather belt, took them in her charge. There was something ominous about this woman. She seemed more suited to a house of correction than this benighted place. She led them up narrow back stairs to a cold bedroom with iron beds and one small window. On each bed was laid out a full set of maid's clothes, complete with pairs of starched drawers.

'Get out of your travelling clothes and get dressed in the uniforms,' said the housekeeper.

She stood to one side of the room, which was lit by a single candle, waiting silently while each girl nervously undressed. They were acutely aware that they would need to be completely naked in front of her. They were conscious that her hard eyes took in every detail of their bodies. In their embarrassment, they hurried to cover themselves. At last they stood dressed.

'Downstairs to the kitchen, where cook will give you supper. You will have no duties tonight except to be inspected by the master and the mistress. You will be called when that is to happen. You will only wear the clothes that are provided for you, including underwear, while you work here,' said the housekeeper.

In the kitchen, the cook fed them well. There were no other staff to be seen. They sat by the fire waiting for the summons. It came at last, and a spotty youth in footman's livery escorted them through long dark corridors. They saw the mistress, Lady Elizabeth, first. She was a most attractive woman in her mid-30s, yet she had something about her that was chilling. She spoke slowly, measuring each word. She started by making the girls turn round and show themselves from all sides. She seemed neither pleased nor displeased with them.

'We are a small household, as we only use part of this wretched house. We have been without maids for a time so there will be much to do to catch up. Mrs Weeks, the housekeeper, will instruct you in such matters. You have come with good references,' she said. 'His Lordship and I have a distrust of young girls. They have their heads in the clouds, run after young men, and do slovenly work. I'm sure you have come from one of those lax and modern homes. London is like that. Here we do things more effectively. Any little failures in your demeanour or duties and we will have Weeks brisk you up in the punishment room. I hope you understand me clearly on that score?'

Alice and Rosemary, bowed their heads, nodded and murmured abject agreements.

'Now his Lordship needs to see over you,' she said. 'Leave now, the boy will show you.'

She turned back to her embroidery.

His Lordship was a swarthy man, not a great deal older that his wife. He was stood in the study by a roaring fire, a full glass and decanter to hand. He waved them in, lined them up before him and contemplated them in silence.

At last he spoke, after slowly sipping from his glass. 'Well, well, well, what do we have here. A couple of prize young hens if ever I've seen a pair. Her Ladyship won't like you two, I'll be bound. Doesn't like attractive young girls. You better get used to her punishment room, she is fond of it. Her and Weeks.'

He sipped again, warming to his task. He asked each their names, making them step forward and give him a little curtsey. Alice and Rosemary relaxed a little and tried to smile.

'I'm going to be blunt, because I'm a blunt man,' he said. 'I like a lot of things, dogs, horses, shooting game, shooting poachers, a little fishing. But in particular, I like a nice young girl. Even better, I like two nice young girls, if you get my drift? I expect you to visit me and accommodate my needs when I send for you. I'll make it plain, it will be part of your duties. You will keep the matter to yourselves and you might as well accept it with good grace and a smile. If you don't, I'll please my wife and send you packing with no references. Worse, I might report you to the constable for theft. Not a pretty set of alternatives. So you be sensible and we will all get along fine.'

His manner hardened as he had moved on to the threats. Alice and Rosemary were dumb struck. Even though they were in no sense worldly, they understood the gist of his Lordship's demands for their additional duties. He had indeed been blunt. All they could do was say

'Yes sir, we will do our best.'

Back in their room with its one candle, they held each other tightly and cried. It was a dreadful place from which they could see there was no escape. Sleep came slowly as their minds dwelt, over and over, upon the events of the evening.

The following day, things seemed a little more normal, though still less than pleasant. The household seemed to consist of the old groom who had been the driver on their arrival. The young lad called Tom, who was footman and everything else. The indifferent cook who kept herself to herself, and the frightening Weeks. There was one other, who kept herself detached from the rest of the servants and that was her ladyship's maid. She was a mature, dowdy woman who spent her time sewing and attending to her ladyship's personal needs. This maid appeared only at meal times and then scuttled off to the upper floors of the house. It was a sad and dark place, bitter as the wind that perpetually blew from the moors above the old house.

Each girl blessed the fact that they had each other, for company and support. Weeks roused them early and set them to doing fires and cleaning grates. Though she was cold, she was reasonable in dealing with their many questions as to where things could be found. She seemed grateful that two hard working pairs of hands had arrived at last.

Alice and Rosemary, lapsed into a tacit acceptance of their lot. The days went by and they soon became used to the place and their duties. Neither master nor mistress seemed to notice them and, except for the occasional instruction, no words passed between them. Even the cook started to make conversation, and the boy Tom, when alone with them, made earnest attempts to please the girls with silly jokes.

One afternoon Rosemary was laying out tea for her ladyship. The silver teapot slipped from her grasp, and fell onto the Turkish rug spraying tea in all directions from lid and spout.

'Stupid child,' said her ladyship. 'Get it cleared up and bring me fresh tea.' That was all she said. Rosemary called for Alice to help, equilibrium was restored and her Ladyship had her tea.

As Rosemary curtseyed before leaving the room, the ominous words came to her ears: 'You'll be brisked up tonight. Now leave.'

Weeks, when told, seemed very detached about the matter. The night came.

'I'm surprised that both of you have made it this far without a visit to the special room my girl,' she said to Rosemary as they walked together up a staircase in the old, unused part of the house. The way was lit by a candle that Weeks held. When they reached the top, a door on the dusty landing stood open and light came from inside. The two of them entered.

The mistress was already there, sitting calmly on a large chair. The room was well lit by wall mounted candles. Rosemary, somewhat in a daze, took in the room. It had once, she saw, been a boudoir. Now it was bare with a few chairs and, in the centre, a wooden construction like a saw-horse but on longer legs. Its top came to an edge which was minimally padded by old, well-stained leather. Each leg fitted with leather straps. Upon one wall, she noticed, there hung an array of instruments of flagellation. Small whips, leather straps and a number of long canes.

'Now girl,' said Weeks. 'Best if you go along with this and get it over with. Just do as I tell you and all will be fine. Slip off your pinafore and dress and be smart about it.'

Rosemary did as she was told, folding the clothes with deliberate neatness onto a chair. She now stood before the two women in her undergarments.

'Have the girl strip to the waist, Weeks, if you please. Don't want her sweating into the good clothes my money provides,' said Lady Elizabeth.

'Off with your top,' said the Housekeeper and Rosemary obeyed, slipping off the simple white chemise to expose her young breasts.

'Have her mount the horse,' said the mistress.

Weeks pulled forward a small wooden box and placed it underneath the horse.

'Climb astride the horse, girl, use the box,' she said.

Rosemary, stood up on the box and swung her leg over the ridge to stand with her legs apart across its edge.

'Come down a little toward the end and then part your drawers and sit down with your bare cunny on the top. I will do the rest,' said Weeks.

Rosemary did as she was told and parted the material to place her sweet place with its brown curls upon the old leather which was marked by the sex of many before her.

Satisfied that the girl was correctly positioned, her bare cunt pressing down against the hard leather top of the saw-horse, Weeks quickly pulled away the box and Rosemary now felt the painful and instant discomfort of the leather forcing open her labia. Quickly Weeks swept up each booted ankle and strapped it high up upon the rear leg of the horse so that Rosemary was seated like a jockey. She then pulled the girl down at the front till her nipples caressed the top of the horse. Each of the girl's wrists was now strapped low down on the front legs. Rosemary was now perfectly placed, bottom up and ready, the edge pressing cruelly on the base of her mound and her clitoris. She now understood the cunning of this sadistic device to add additional suffering and pain.

Weeks proceeded to bare the bottom. She pulled open the division of the drawers and worked the material back, tucking it under so that each neat, tightened cheek was clearly on show and gleaming pink in the candle light.

'Now Week's, there's a good sight. What a suitable bottom the young Miss has. Well rounded and pert, ripe for a brisking. Such fresh young skin, neglected for so long. We must make her do her duties without carelessness. A good cane, Weeks, best for a tight little bottom. That one, the third from the end. That will get her working on the horse, give her a good ride.'

It was the first time that her Ladyship had shown any sign of animation or interest. Her cheeks had something of a flush and her languid voice had become excited. Weeks took up the suggested cane and flexed it a few times to get its measure. She then positioned herself to use it on the proffered bottom. While this had been going on, Rosemary had tried to keep quiet, but the growing pain between her legs had made her whimper.

'Two dozen if you please, Weeks, we must make up for neglect and mark that virgin skin a little. Keep them in a tight group, she has a small arse. Not too hurried, strike just below the curve, you know the spot I'm sure. Now off you go.'

Rosemary had known the burning pain of the birch on many occasions during her time in the orphanage. That was a long time ago and while the birch twigs had been painful, they in no way matched the extraordinary pain of each stroke of the cane. Weeks was obviously skilled at this task and laid the strokes one upon another to the lower part of the rounded cheeks. At each stroke Rosemary could not help but drive forward and punish her crotch. 'Working upon the horse,' as the Mistress had said. After a number of strokes, Rosemary started to shudder and the muscles of her buttocks engaged in involuntary spasms. With each whistle of the cane, and its frightening crack upon the naked flesh came the attendant, pitiful scream of the punished girl. The pause between strokes was full of heavy breathing and sobs.

Lady Elizabeth sat upright upon her chair, hands tightly clasped, rocking slowly with ill-concealed delight as the beating progressed. Her eyes were fixed and bright, looking intensely upon the scene, relishing, quite unashamedly, this act of sadism. There was clear disappointment when the allotted number strokes were finished. She quickly rose from her chair and left the room.

'The girl may have two days off to let the bleeding stop before she goes back to work. We do not want her garments soiled,' she said, as she left.

Rosemary was near fainting, sobbing uncontrollably, unable to support her body any longer. Weeks, methodically wiped the cane on a cloth before hanging it back on its hook on the wall.

Alice did her best to comfort her friend when they were alone in their bedroom. She was distressed when shown what she was familiar with as a sweet posterior to kiss and caress. It was now a black and purple bottom with the raised ridges of the wheals through which little drops of blood still seeped. Weeks had provided an old towel for the girl to protect the bed clothes, though there was no chance of her lying bottom down for some time to come.

Alice knew that it would be only a short period before Lady Elizabeth found a spurious reason to break in another girl to the ways of her house. And so she was even more careful to apply herself to her own duties, especially as she had a double load to accommodate for a few days to come. Three days later, Rosemary was up and about again, though still very much in pain from the rubbing of her clothing. On that third night both maids were summoned late to attend the master.

His Lordship was again in his study, warming by the fire and sipping brandy. He was dressed now in a long quilted dressing gown that hung down to his slippered feet. When Tom had shut the door behind them, he waved them forward to come close to him.

'Which of you two pretty things had to visit my wife's little play room?' he asked.

'It was Rosemary,' said Alice, pointing to her friend.

'Ah, yes indeed,' said his Lordship. 'It would be you first, the little, slim, shy one. Just her Ladyship's taste I'm sure. Now Rosemary, be a good girl and slip off your dress, so that I may see what sort of job Weeks did. Come girl, off with your dress.'

Alice looked horrified and Rosemary went quite white, though she started the process of undressing, there being no alternative but to comply with her Master. As the garments were removed she placed them on a chair until she stood before his Lordship in her white underclothes. He turned to Alice.

'You there girl, what's your name?'

'Alice, sir,' said Alice.

'Yes, Alice. Nice name for a wench. Keep your friend company and slip off your dress as well. I like to compare a fresh bottom with one that's incurred her Ladyship's interests. Come girl don't hesitate, get off that dress.'

Alice, reddened, yet had no alternative but to do as she was told. His Lordship now watched the more curvaceous Alice undress down to her underwear. He now had them both innocently posed before him. He savoured the moment and sipped his drink, nodding in appreciation.

'See that table there.' He pointed to a massive oak table on one side of the room. ' Both of you be good girls and oblige me by going to that table and bending yourselves over it.'

Then as an after thought he added, 'Just to make things pleasant, both slip off your tops, so that I have the pleasure of inspecting you there. I like to see the cut of my young female servants.'

One button at a time, Rosemary and Alice slowly undid their cheap, cotton tops. They slipped them off and let the warm yellow light of the candles play across their breasts. Rosemary's were smaller and tipped up to form dark cheeky ends. Alice's were full and round with large, pink areolas and soft nipples.

'There's a fine sight, something for all tastes. I'll come to those in a while but for now, bend over the table for me.' The two maids did as they were told, resting their warm bosoms upon the cold wood.

The Master rose from his armchair and approached the pair of knickered posteriors. He went first to Alice and after a moment's hesitation, slipped both his hands into the division of her tightened drawers. He slowly pulled them open, exposing the naked flesh beneath. When both cheeks were on show, he felt them with the palms of his hands, caressing their firmness. Without a word, he now moved to Rosemary and repeated the same thing. This time, he traced the wheals and wounds with his fingertips, pressing until he made the girl cry out a little.

'Nothing like a good, heavy cane for a young girl's rump. That cold-hearted vixen Weeks surely knows her trade with such an implement. What a neat small arse you have, girl, almost like a boy's.' His fingers edged between the division of Rosemary's cheeks and a finger pushed into her puckered hole.

'Nice and tight. What a pleasure that will be.'

He stepped back. 'Up you get a moment. Alice, you stay down.' Rosemary stood up and turned to face him.

'Let's have a look at these titties.'

He now proceeded to feel each breast in turn. The cold table had hardened her nipples so that they stood up. He lingered, tweaking each teat in turn between his finger and his thumb, while Rosemary shivered a little, head bowed, not daring to look him in the eye. She was then told to resume her bent over position and he turned his attention to Alice. She now had her breasts examined and teased. At last she also was returned to the table. His Lordship left them there while he went to a small cabinet, from which he withdrew a jar. Putting the jar down between them, he now reached round, beneath the waist and undid the cord tie of Rosemary's knickers. This done, he eased them down. She was now full exposed and naked.

'Part your legs, shy little Rosemary,' he said.

She obeyed, shuffling her black boots on the carpet until her legs were as open as far as her drawers permitted.

'Good girl, sensible to be obedient.'

From within his dressing gown, his Lordship now exposed his erect penis. It stood out, its large head glinting in the light, already a little wet. Rosemary knew nothing of this development but remained frozen in fear over the table. The master fingered Rosemary's cunt. Finding it wet between the curls, he smiled with approval and dipped the head of his prick in the moist nest and pulled it out well lubricated. He now opened the jar and applied the oily cream, working it into the maid's anus. Satisfied, he wet himself again and then rubbed his penis tip against the girl's rear passage. With one forceful thrust of his hips he entered her. Rosemary, arched her back and cried out with surprise and pain, as her nerves fired up with this sudden intrusion. He took no notice but pulled aside his dressing gown to expose his own naked body and then entered Rosemary fully, until his balls banged against the rear of her vulva. The girl screamed, as his body, at each impact, punished again her bruised buttocks.

He reached forward and grabbed her breasts, one in each hand. As his hips pounded he tortured the small bosom with harsh squeezing fingers, stretching and twisting the tender nipples. His body bent over her, kept her upon the table which provide an unyielding edge to her thighs so that there was no reprieve from the deep penetration.

When her cries became weaker and her movements calmer, he at last withdrew, letting her naked form sink slowly down to the floor. Alice had witnessed this sodomising of her dear friend. She had not known what to do. And fear of this man kept her from trying to intervene. His Lordship, though, reasserted his authority and gave two hard slaps to Alice's bottom. He stripped down her knickers as he had done with Rosemary and, far more harshly forced his fingers deep into her sex.

'You're the proud one with spirit, not yet curbed by a taste of the cane. What a nice cunt you have, all wet and dripping, soaking and greedy. I hope you didn't think I would leave you out of the fun. What a fine arse, so round, plenty of space for a dog whip. I'll suggest it to her Ladyship.'

He slapped her cheeks again to emphasise his point, leaving red hand prints. His fingers pushed inside again, making Alice squeal and cry.

'Still a little virgin I see, so tight up there for my tool.'

Grabbing Alice's hips, he forced himself into her sex. It parted and opened till he was against the flesh of her bottom. With rhythmic strokes he took her, hurting her breasts as he had done to Rosemary, and enjoying her cries and protestations. He did not come inside her, for he did not want to risk her becoming pregnant. Instead he withdrew and sprayed his seed across her bottom and bare back.

Time passed, and the girls fell into a dark routine. It was as though the house, and the wild moor above, broke their youthful and innocent nature, to replace it instead with one of grudging acceptance of their lot. For they were after all slaves in a world of absolute power. Their bottoms toughened to the cane and their private places accepted the entry of their Lord and master. Knowing as he did, that one or other of them would suffer again as he beat his hips against their freshly punished bottom.

As one once remarked to the other, in the world as it was, it would be much worse if they did not have a domestic position. As long as they pleased, they would keep their jobs as maids and wear their smart white aprons. They were therefore both determined to please both mistress and master. On that they were very clear.

VIII   THE VISITORS

*I*n a police state, somewhere during the 20th century, lived a very infamous and cruel member of the State police. His private pleasure was a young, intelligent university student who had been arrested for anti-state activities. This man had taken a personal fancy to the young woman and after systematically breaking her had rebuilt her mind to serve his whim. It was a classic Stockholm syndrome experiment, the girl now believing that the man was her saviour and the only person capable of helping her back to normality. It is a sad, very disturbing tale of humiliation and degradation, even her speech has become dysfunctional and childlike. As happens so often in such cases they had developed a bizarre and unhealthy symbiosis, a warped form of love, perhaps?

❋ ❋ ❋

*E*leanor was very excited. She was also very nervous. The Doctor had just called her to his private apartments and explained to her most carefully that he was going to be entertaining some of his important friends that evening. Now that she existed, as he described to her eager face, which even occasionally dared to look up into his, he felt that she could be present at the gathering. Further he suggested that she could be of actual use, serving drinks and passing round plates of canapés to his guests. What had made her really bubble with a rare joy, was that he showed her a pretty lace apron and a little lace cap that he had decided she should wear over her chemise. She was, as has also been said, intensely nervous; for he had reminded her that she should be on her very best behaviour at all times. The voice he had used when he said that was his 'dark voice' and that was a tone of voice she knew so very well.

"You will wash your chemise and you will wash yourself, you may, as always, use my bath and bathroom. See also that you shave your sexual parts well and your armpits. I don't want my guests to smell your regrettably disgusting, sexual odours, Eleanor."

"No dear kind Doctor Mueller... wretched deviant whore wash her parts... shave all the bits dear kind Doctor Mueller... be very clean for important persons who visit... dear kind Doctor Mueller."

The absence of the word 'cunt' which she hated being made to say, from her answer earned her a sanction, as he called it, from his crop.

When she had finished whimpering from the intense pain of six strokes and carefully pulled down her chemise, she tried again.

"Wash... shave wretched deviants whore's cun...t... dear kind Doctor Mueller... thank you dear kind Doctor Mueller for teaching wretched deviant whore... to talk right... say difficult word cun..t dear kind Doctor Mueller."

"I fear it is a slow process Eleanor." Mueller leaned back and sighed, still fingering his crop. "A very slow process, still my essential instrument is always to hand, isn't it Eleanor?"

"Yes dear kind Doctor Mueller... nice crop good teacher wretched deviant whore... dear kind Doctor Mueller...punish wretched deviant whore's bad places, bad person... teach me say... dear kind Doctor Mueller."

Mueller smiled a rare smile as his living project hung her head and mumbled the words. He liked an excuse to punish her. With his normal desire for precision he always aimed carefully using the strap at the end of his crop, often though his little broken bird would wriggle in anticipation of pain at the last moment and spoil his aim; so frustrating to his sense of total control. It was though he mused, always just a spontaneous punishment for her small failings.

Little Eleanor set about the tasks that she had been set with unnatural enthusiasm. She washed her filthy chemise, being most careful not to tear the fragile material. To do so would she knew incur perhaps a lengthy time hanging naked after the long application of his thin whip or even the frightening rigors of the dreadful, dark pain whip.

She was pleased with her sad efforts to get the dismal thing clean and free from its filthy stains and hung the cloth to dry by the Doctor's big stove in the kitchen. Naturally, she was quite naked, having nothing else to wear, but then that state didn't normally bother her for she was used to appearing so whenever the good, kind Doctor needed to attend to her body in some instructive way or conduct an intimate examination.

She could, with her heightened sense of awareness, hear him in his study and she slipped up to his bathroom to run a bath. Washing was a luxury he seldom afforded her as he preferred her body and in particular her sex to smell. She always smelt very strongly around the time of her period, not that she always had one these days due to her poor diet. He, with his normal humiliating cruelty, denied her any means of coping with the menstrual blood that would flow; so she had to use her long suffering chemise, pulled embarrassingly between her legs. This of course in turn became caked with her dried discharge.

"You're a dirty little thing, aren't you, Eleanor?" He would sometimes comment looking at the stains upon her one piece of clothing.

She would hang her head, embarrassed at his comments. Deep down inside she wanted to be clean, wanted to wear clothes like the women in the magazines she looked at when he wasn't there. She didn't like to smell, to smell herself, to smell her fingers after masturbation, to know that the paper she was permitted to use after defecation did not really clean that place; for when she was given helpful liquids his frequent remedy for any sign of constipation, he would also comment upon that to her total mortification.

If he was though in a very good mood or her pubic hair had grown too long or even he couldn't stand the stench, he sometimes told her to 'scuttle off' and wash and shave herself and the chemise. If not she would have to live with her own filth for days on end.

Eleanor carefully arranged a razor from the Doctor's collection on the side of the bath and with real pleasure climbed in and let herself sink into the healing, hot, steaming water. She luxuriated in the feel and smell of his expensive Parisian soap upon her skin, massaging the rich lather into every nook of her body. It was a strange paradox even to her befuddled mind, that on one hand he let her stay so filthy but on the other encouraged her to use his facilities to the full when he decided she should be clean. However she was well aware that good kind Doctor Mueller had many strange ways she couldn't ever begin to understand.

Then with care she started to shave the course stubble that had grown upon her mound and lips and under her arms. She was careful when shaving her right armpit as the tips of the thin whip had recently left their cuts there during a morning whipping, with her face down on his bed. Still it was pure bliss to be clean and to be shaved. She rubbed the soap into her matted hair, trying to tease out the small tangles, for bald as he was Mueller never had any shampoo. It was wonderful to be clean, wonderful to exist. Doctor Mueller was so very kind and caring to her and she was immensely grateful. How kind he was to have made her as his little broken bird. To spend so much time trying to heal her broken wings so that one day she could become real again and fly. How kind he was to let her be clean.

"Dear kind Doctor Mueller." She muttered quietly to herself as she lay there in the water. "Dear, dear, kind Doctor Mueller."

Early that evening, she cautiously went to his office as she had been directed and he had her stand right in front of him and slowly inspected her, even sniffed her. She was wearing again the clean and dry chemise. His hand playfully ruffled her hair and she almost purred with pleasure at this gentle attention. She loved his kind touch.

"Judging by the smell filling my office I will have nothing left of my expensive, French soap my little broken bird." Again he smiled and stroked her head. Eleanor had rarely seen him in such a good mood. She reasoned that the imminent coming of his visitors was to prove a great pleasure for him.

"I not use much....special.... cost much.....soap dear kind Doctor Mueller..... wretched deviant whore..... careful not use much... special soap.... still much left, wretched deviant whore got.....very small.....tiny..... body not need much soap, shave armpits and cun..t dear kind Doctor Mueller wash chemise...... all clean now as told to....... dear kind Doctor Mueller."

"No, no, no my little broken bird, I'm sure you didn't. After all we have to have you looking at you best for my visitors don't we and I think you have done a very fine job so I'm extremely pleased. Now let us see what you look like in your new maids uniform shall we?"

At this he reached first for the apron and handed it to her trembling little hands.

With great care and ceremony she slipped the halter over her head and tied the cords of the apron around her slim waits. He next passed over the little maids white cap, frilly with its lace to her and again and she carefully applied it to her bent head.

Eleanor now stood there uncertain of and even fearing his reaction to her new form of dress. She fiddled with her chemise and shuffled from one foot to the other making little sounds. He looked upon the transformation with his normal cold and discerning stare. He was pleased with what he saw. A dreadful parody of a maid, a humiliating parody, how pleasing.

His child, his Eleanor, her hair all roughly cropped, wild tuffs popping out from around the hat, the crisp, lace edged apron in such contrast to the patched and stained chemise beneath. Long, lean legs appearing, to end in bare feet, feet he had beaten so cruelly on occasions. Her thin, muscular arms and tiny wrists, the agile, expressive hands grasping the hem of the chemise and always constantly in a nervous motion. Above all, her hunched and cowed posture, head to the ground, eyes never daring to meet his. Yes she would do splendidly, such a visual amusement for his friends to ridicule. What added to his pleasure was that she was completely unaware of just how ridiculous she looked; instead he could detect that she was actually thrilled with her new appearance.

He took the happy Eleanor to his kitchen and showed her the plates of canapés that his chef had carefully prepared and left ready. He then showed her the bottles of wine opened and left to breathe for the drinks and the set of fine, bright, clean crystal goblets. She took the matter very seriously as she did the cleaning of his instruments and his Doctor's white coat. At every instruction she bobbed up and down in her outfit and mumbled an incoherent…"Yes dear kind Doctor Mueller." Mueller continued to beam.

In no time there was the sound of a large official car on the drive and Mueller rushed off to greet his favoured guests. To Eleanor who loitered with eager anticipation in the main hall, they were, much to her sudden distress, a most frightening group. Two tall, arrogant members of the State police in their full, black dress uniforms each accompanied by an equivalent State police woman, also in their uniform of white shirt, black tie, black, tight breaches and polished, black leather boots. Young, blond females with their hair set in a conforming, tight bun.

The men were of equal rank to Mueller and quite obviously old friends of his, the younger women were of course their mistresses and they hung back a little in the presence of the infamous Doctor. After much loud conversation and boisterous greetings which caused Eleanor to shrink into the shadows, the party moved into Mueller's sitting room. Eleanor was at first at a loss as to what to do and hung back in the hall. Then much to her consternation the distinctive voice of the Doctor loudly called her name.

Slowly, with halting steps, she made her way into the lounge, which was already thick with cigarette smoke its occupants all seated around the large, low, central table. As Eleanor entered the conversation stopped abruptly and they all looked at her. Eleanor shuffled in her head as low as her bent shoulders would permit. One of the women started to giggle, the others looked on in surprised bewilderment.

"Mueller!" exclaimed one of the officers. "Don't tell me that the annoying shortages have reduced you to finding your servants from the streets, or worse, the camps?" The others laughed.

The Doctor, looking most serious, held up his hand to quell the ripples of laughter that still flowed around the room.

"Ladies, Gentlemen, do prey be serious for a moment." His authoritative tone silenced the room in seconds.

"We must not laugh at this poor young girl, tut, tut, shame upon you. For I would like to introduce you to my special, personal project. She is called Eleanor. She has, as you can see, done her very best for us tonight, washed her chemise, late of Paris, and even washed herself, so that she can help me by waiting upon us without your having to smell her normal, rather pungent odour."

Eleanor had tears in her eyes for she had tried her best and the laughter and words hurt her deeply. All her joy and pride in her appearance had withered in that one moment.

At that comment, there were more restrained giggles from the women and smirks upon the faces of the men. Mueller however continued with his pretence at seriousness. He noticed Eleanor's tears.

"Eleanor, please don't sniffle, blow your nose on your chemise, you didn't expect them to find a person who is not actually real beautiful, how silly of you?"

Eleanor dragged up a piece of cloth and blew her nose noisily.

"This is no ordinary person." he continued. "This is the young woman who has been helping me so diligently with my experiments into personality alteration. You have all heard me speak of this most interesting work or read my papers on it I'm sure?"

"Ah," spoke up an officer, "yes, you have written upon this little project of yours. So... this is her? Well, well, how very interesting, Mueller."

The others stared at Eleanor with renewed curiosity. Eleanor though almost hopped from one foot to the other with distress, desperate to be excused.

"Eleanor?" enquired Mueller. "Would you be so very kind and

helpful and bring a glass of wine for each of my guests? Do it carefully. Then when each of us has a drink, you can hand round the canapés. Off you go now."

Eleanor gratefully backed carefully out of the room to rush into the kitchen. One at a time she slowly served them each with a glass, carrying them with both hands as a child might, so as not to spill a drop. The smiles on the faces of the guests had turned to looks of fascination as each in turn was served. The strangely dressed creature before them would nod her head and give a little bob when she passed the glass over with exaggerated care. They in turn, at a loss as how to respond, thanked her with false solemnity.

She served Doctor Mueller last and when he had his glass she looked around the room to, it seems, ascertain if she had served all present.

"I done... all glasses. All have glass... dear kind Doctor Mueller."

"Yes Eleanor, well done, now bring in some plates of canapés for my guests if you will."

She bobbed again and fled back to the kitchen happy now at being useful, needed.

"It's quite remarkable Doctor." said one of the women. "Is she always so bent over or does she have a deformity?"

"No deformity, just a text book example of abject submission to any authority. She dare not stand erect and look any one in the eye. In fact I would have to punish her if she did that without permission. For a long time I created the situation, the delusion where, in her mind, she did not exist unless in my presence. It is a psychological pathology that is totally destructive to the id. She is now much happier as I have granted her existence again but much as she does crave it, not the right to become a 'real' person, so to speak. One takes and one gives, one controls."

Mueller smiled to his small and attentive audience enthused by their obvious interest, explaining further his techniques and methods as though the cowed and withdrawn Eleanor was not even in the room. They hung on his every word and at each new revelation, stared even harder at Eleanor as though she was a prize exhibit in a funfair. She continued to wander the room, thrusting a plate of canapés under any nose she could find, except the Doctor's. She was, as always, frightened to get too close to him without being asked to.

The questions now came thick and fast as they admired his terrifying prodigy and of course marvelled at his dreadful cruelty.

"Eleanor, I think my guests have had enough canapés for now, leave the dishes on the table and fetch a bottle of wine and go round and top up their glasses, it seems our discussion here is thirsty work."

Again he beamed with pride and Eleanor jumped at hearing her name and rushed from the room to get the wine.

Mueller now finished off the conversation on Eleanor.

"Enough for now, for I am instead most interested in hearing your news and how you are dealing with such a rush of saboteurs and dissidents. Such problems you seem to have as though the world was going mad and so many deluded people were anxious to frequent our cold, inhospitable cellars. However a little later we will return to the subject of my Eleanor and I will show you some interesting features of my little project."

The last comment was said with that hint of the coldness that Mueller was famous for having at the Centre. The women noticed this and withdrew just a little.

Eleanor dutifully served wine and the evening became quite

convivial. At last Mueller signalled Eleanor to come to him and she was instructed to curl up at his feet. His hand reached down and gently stroked and tugged at the hair on the back of her head, though she was grateful for his attentions and nuzzled into his legs, she detected a less that comforting signal in his touch that made her feel distinctly apprehensive.

One of the officers commented upon the tranquil scene that they presented to the group.

"She is like a fucking dog with you Mueller, quite like a pet. What a difference from our world. You are a man… full of surprises. Tell me, if you pardon the question, have you or do you use the woman sexually? She has quite a sweet and desirable body it seems and is, as you have explained, of good stock. I assume that she was well and harshly assaulted upon her arrest?"

At this, one of the women, now slightly drunk giggled openly.

"You know Freitag," answered Mueller, "you are quite incorrigible. You are well aware that my methods, even at the Centre, do not support your more direct and violent applications. She has been spared normal beatings even at the time of her arrest as she was also, upon my clear instruction, spared the usual repeated assaults. This was for the very reason that I had decided that she might prove to be the project I was seeking. As to my personal involvement with her I do not have your constant, lustful needs, Wolf."

With this he pointed to Freitag's most attractive consort, who had now removed her uniform tie and had undone her white blouse by some buttons so to expose the tops of her round, young breasts; the nipples clearly erect through the thin material.

"No, Wolf, for me to use her body for my pleasure would have been quite wrong, desirable as she may be. She believes…"

And he paused to caress and look down into Eleanor's lean face.

"She believes, due to my careful programming, that she was a whore and sold her body to raise money for her anti-state cause. Of course, in such circumstances, I couldn't possibly be seen by her to be intimate, it would have, as you will understand, altered the dynamics. After all, as you well know, I have my private recourses for such pleasures. I do however work her tight and inexperienced vagina with a suitable penis-like implement if I wish to reward her, something she finds of course most pleasurable but intensely degrading, she wriggles quite beautifully when aroused and deeply penetrated."

"Eleanor." He looked down at her again. "Please tell my guests what you name is."

Eleanor, squirmed her head against the Doctor's leg in a shy response.

"Eleanor." His hand pulled harshly at the hair on her head, and his voice trucked no dissent from her.

"Eleanor, please stand up and tell my guests your name."

Slowly she got to her feet and now tugging and kneading at the lace edge of the apron, she did as she was instructed.

"I'm the wretched… deviant whore… NF-713… dear kind Doctor Mueller."

The words were mumbled and the Doctor asked her to repeat what she had said, but much louder.

Again she made her embarrassing statement and the audience smiled indulgently.

"Eleanor, I fear that you were being very silly, even childish over this simple matter. First you have to be told twice to make your statement, then you mumbled it and again had to be told to repeat yourself, didn't you?"

She shuffled around and hung her head.

"Yes, dear kind Doctor Mueller."

Mueller turned to the people.

"I'm sorry that my subject is not performing efficiently this evening, she is normally far better behaved and responsive to instructions. Just why she is so unresponsive even sullen I can only attribute to your presence. It's true that she is not used to behaving correctly in sophisticated company such as yours. I have found it always to be the best thing when any little failing occurs, to apply prompt and effective correction. One must never let even small slips pass unnoticed."

"Oh Doctor, I know you are noted for your exacting demands." They all laughed at this obvious comment. "But surely the poor young woman is just overwhelmed by it all. Making her say that was really very cruel of you Mueller, no wonder she mumbled," said Freitag.

They, in the good spirits of the moment, laughed again, even Mueller smiled a wry smile.

"Since when, Wolf my friend, have the State police been speaking up in the defence of detainees? Is life in the torture chambers making you soft – or perhaps you just fancy the girl?" suggested Mueller.

Eleanor simply stood there, swaying slightly and looking fixedly at her bare feet as this banter passed around her confused head.

Mueller now turned to the other officer, Heilmann.

"My dear Matthias, you have teenage daughters, what do you do when they misbehave?"

"Well, if I'm at home and not in my 'torture' chamber," (more laughter) "and one of them gets up to mischief – which seems to be quite often – why, then they are soon over my knee, their knickers at their knees and my hand goes to work. Thank you

Papa they say politely when they have a red bottom. That sort of disciplining soon gets their attention."

Mueller smiled again. "What an excellent remedy Matthias. As you seem such an expert on recalcitrant young females, perhaps you would oblige me by demonstrating your skills upon the silly young Eleanor here. I think it would be most entertaining for us all!"

At this suggestion there was a general nodding of slightly inebriated approval, especially from the women.

"Eleanor!" commanded Mueller, turning to address her as she jumped at the sound of her name.

"Be so kind as to go to Herr Heilman and bend over his lap."

Heilman smiled at the Doctor. "You really want me to spank her on her bottom, Mueller?"

"Oh yes, Matthias, I think we would all like that and Eleanor would be reminded of her manners at the same time, so please feel free my friend," answered Mueller.

Heilmann beckoned Eleanor and she went over to him. With practiced ease he bent her slim, unresisting body, over his knee. Then in a leisurely way he pulled up the old chemise to reveal to everyone her neat, round, bare cheeks.

"What, no knickers for the girl! Mueller, you are a mean man! She is after all a *real* little whore. I shall enjoy this."

Eleanor knew what was to happen for dear kind Doctor Mueller sometimes did this when he was in a good, relaxed mood and she had been silly. However she had never been touched for correction by another before. She wished in her heart that she had some knickers, like a real person would, but then she thought of course that she was just a whore. Her complicated thoughts were brought to an abrupt end as Heilmann's firm hand came down onto her tight skin. As the spanking progressed, Eleanor squirmed delightfully and the others even started to clap in time to Heilmanns's rhythm, all except the Doctor, who looked upon the proceedings in a detached way.

Eleanor's flesh became exceptionally red and finally Heilmann stopped and told Eleanor to get up. They could all see that she was crying, little tears running down her cheeks and catching the light. Mueller was, however, unmoved.

"Thank you Matthias, I'm sure that served its purpose, especially as I require her to perform a further little demonstration for you all.

"Eleanor, now that the kind officer has treated you like the silly girl that you are some times, you must redeem yourself and demonstrate your obedience to my wishes. I think we should show my guests a little more of your self, I'm sure you would like to do that?"

He now addressed them with his usual desire to entertain.

"Eleanor has always been a prudish young woman, she came from a strict religious home and I am doubtful if she has ever had a proper sexual experience, though she had a boyfriend and she was not a virgin when I first examined her. She is therefore particularly embarrassed concerning her sex. It would be good training for her discipline if she was made to show it to strangers and further if they actually examined it."

He turned to Eleanor.

"Eleanor, since my guests are most interested in such things I would like you to lift up your chemise and go and stand in front of each of them in turn, part your legs and thrust out your sex to them. Then tell each of them what that place of yours is called. They may wish to touch you and examine you there, so you will stand very still and behave." He waved his hand to the group.

"Do please feel free to examine her quite delightful genitals, they are very clean though she may have lubricated, something she does constantly."

Eleanor started to tremble but in fear of sanctions she slowly and carefully walked up to Heilmann again and stood very close to him, tears still in her wet eyes. Then with both hands she slowly pulled up her chemise and adopted the posture that the Doctor had told her to. In a small, frightened voice she explained what she was showing to the man.

"This my... wretched deviant whore's c...un...t. It is the centre of all my badness, dear kind Visitor."

The officer, though he had seen a multitude of prisoners' genitals, and most recently Eleanor's from behind, was, because of the strange circumstances, still totally intrigued. He leant forward and peered closely at the shaven sex. Then with infinite care, as one might touch a rare orchid, he put down his glass and with the index fingers of both hands pulled aside the proffered labia.

"Mueller, Mueller, what a real, fucking evil devil you are. How can you encourage us to humiliate this girl. However, intrigued by Eleanor's passivity and the novelty of the situation he continued his detailed examination, even inserting a finger. She's a tight little whore, isn't she, Mueller?" He chuckled as his finger moved to caress the exposed purple bud, well erected from the massive dose of aphrodisiacs the Doctor had given Eleanor earlier that evening. At this touch Eleanor's whole body shuddered and twisted in response and fluid trickled from her. Heilmann encouraged, persisted with his intimate examination of the clitoris.

"Amazing! Quite amazing! And doesn't the girl drip? It is also so unusually large and distended, has something been done?"

"Oh yes, Heilmann, you are, as always, observant. I provide

her with medication that heightens her sexual libido so that she must masturbate constantly, which over time increases the size of that small but essential organ, leaving it permanently aroused. Of course such procedures reinforce her belief in her history as a whore and keep her body exhausted from repeated orgasms. It also fosters and generates a package of total degradation."

Eleanor's embarrassing anguish was complete and she went beyond the little tears and started to sob silently, just her shoulders shaking, She had also unfortunately not urinated for a very long time, having been distracted by her new duties. Suddenly, to her intense humiliation, she could hold her bursting bladder no longer and a stream of warm urine gushed from her urethra.

Heilmann moved back quickly to avoid being soaked and burst into uncontrolled laughing, as did the others with the exception of the Doctor who, anger welling in him, shouted at Eleanor to get to a toilet. Tears streaming down her face she rushed from the room.

His guests found the occasion hilarious. They were all completely familiar with detainees pissing themselves from pain or fear ,especially female onrd, and to see it happen on the famous Doctor's carpet was great entertainment.

Spluttering apologies Mueller got up and left the room to find Eleanor. He found her crouching under his stairs in her nest. His anger had become cold and as she crept out at his bidding she was contorted with dreadful fear. He savagely grabbed the scruff of her hair and dragged her back into the room. Their in front of his startled guests, he ripped the cap from her head and instructed her to strip. She obeyed as promptly as she could, almost tearing the piss soaked chemise from herself.

"Ladies and Gentlemen, I hope that you will indulge me but my project requires a little lesson in manners."

He left Eleanor, a naked, cowering bundle on the floor with excited and stimulated conversation flying across the room fully encouraged by the amount they had all drunk. What a night they were having, Mueller never failed to entertain. One of the women even leant forward and poked the trembling form that was Eleanor with her finger.

Mueller soon returned carrying a small surgical tray upon which lay both a speculum and a freshly filled glass syringe with a long menacing needle. Eleanor's eyes widened in real terror and she shrank away, for she knew their intended purpose so very well. Mueller turned to the group.

"Please pay close attention, you may all find this most instructive. Instinctively the two women shuddered a little as Mueller pulled on his latex gloves.

IX   THE CANDLE

LUCILLE WAS AGAIN IN A WORLD SHE FEARED yet also craved and adored. This was for her Griselda's world, a place, a time, where always Griselda was in charge, where this woman would always exact full payment for fulfilling Lucille's dreams. Fearful though she always was, Lucille could never avoid returning. Deep, now fully implanted in her very soul was an insatiable craving. She always hated the actual price that was necessary, never could understand why she submitted to such treatment, but afterwards… now that was a very different feeling. Afterwards she always needed to return, to find that place again, for she was left with a feeling of such rare pleasure that was so utterly essential to repeatedly experience.

Lucille knew so little about Griselda, in a way ignorance of this figure increased the attendant mystery, fuelled the attraction as the unknown always does, it seems. Lucille had to make the required appointment, the choice was hers and hers alone, and lifting that phone from its cradle was the greatest challenge. For days, even weeks she would put off the moment, her insides crawling with the fingers of indecision. Time and time again the bakelite handset rested in her hand with the insistent, impatient, shrill voice of the operator asking for the number. Always, with mumbled apologies, she would let the receiver drop again and hear the click of disconnection from the earpiece. In the end her need would overcome her fears and she would give the operator that significant number and during the brief and clipped conversation make an appointment.

The sexual exchange between a dominant and a submissive is fairly commonplace. However, what changed the dynamics for Lucille was that she knew that she would be watched and watched by men who paid for that illicit entertainment. Griselda had once explained that the real attraction for her clients was that she was a woman with a woman – always a matter of interest to the male – and that this also permitted the watching eyes and minds not to feel jealously that a man was usurping their fantasised place.

They were there, yet unseen, each with their own personal one-way mirror. An anonymous audience. Old, young, eager, discerning, acquaintances or even treasured friends. Lucille would never know who she performed for, nor know their reactions. It was for her like a brightly lit stage with the audience beyond the pit, there, but hidden by the darkness. Unlike the theatre she would not even have the approbation of applause, no way to measure, so she would always strive to give her best, to go beyond her best, lest she disappoint.

In her mind she pictured them even as Griselda worked upon her, it helped her to cope, somewhere to escape to. She could see them, breathing perhaps a little harder, their eyes reluctant to even blink at special moments. A hand, absentmindedly touching themselves, feeling their hardness. There would also, she knew, be the cold, detached experts, the connoisseurs; critical perfectionists who would tut beneath their breaths if she failed in any way, or, she desperately hoped, nod with knowledgeable approval on occasions.

Lucille also knew that she was very lucky, for Griselda had most precise and exacting standards and many were rejected. Griselda had at their first meeting remarked that she had just the pure, English mature beauty her clients appreciated. When she had undressed for the woman and had been examined, her bottom had been found most suitable, of the required shape and texture to withstand corporal pain for long and demanding periods. It also seemed that things like legs, stomachs, genitals and breasts were equally suitable. It was the most perfect of praise she had ever received for she knew that it had been coldly critical and methodical, for gratuitous flattery was something Griselda did not practice.

She always remembered the arousal that had grown within her, sensations she had never ever known before, when the examination become intimate and thorough. The different position she had to adopt that had humiliated and embarrassed her. Worst of all – the final necessary test to measure and judge her fresholds and ability to cope with punishment. Beyond tentative experiments with a few past men, which had at least confirmed her suspicions about what would really drive her needs, Lucille had never experienced the requirements of Griselda's professional world. When the test had commenced, it was only the greater obstacle of humiliation that prevented her from quitting and rushing from Griselda's presence. She has only managed to cope by telling herself that she had already managed to cope thus far and that logically it would eventually come to an end.

Of course it did have an ending and she had knelt, rather than sat and had gratefully taken the proffered glass of cold champagne. It wasn't so much relief that she felt at that moment but rather an extraordinary pride. Also the erotic rush of a burning fantasy at last fulfilled was all-consuming. It was because of both that very first moment, together with the extraordinary feelings that engulfed her when it was over, that she constantly felt the need to return to and to find it again. Griselda had cautioned her against visiting her too often. It seemed, upon a technical note, that the innocence of her flesh was a great asset. That it marked so dramatically and pleasingly, something her secreted guests would delight in. How her inevitable bruises appeared even before the end to enhance the drama and underline so visually the severity that was craved by those who paid or were chosen to be present. As Griselda had eloquently remarked as her fingers caressed her handiwork…

"A beautiful, perfect bottom with silken, tight, pale skin set upon elegant, long, well-muscled thighs… this intriguing picture then expertly worked upon until finally humiliatingly displayed for all to admire the inevitable desecration of such perfection. Now that, young lady, is what you will bring so charmingly to my little parties."

For Lucille, such flattery sealed their bond. The need to please through her suffering was paramount.

✳ ✳ ✳

So it was that Lucille once more entered Griselda's special room. It was opulent to an extreme in a strange, bizarre taste. One wall consisted of the mirrors behind which sat her clients; small perforations, cleverly hidden behind the gilded wall candle holders, permitted the essential sounds of the room to be heard. The opposite wall was one huge mirror as one might find in a dance studio. Its purpose was to reflect the hidden aspects of any figures in the room back to the admirers so that no matter what position was adopted very little would escape, especially the facial expressions of the supplicants or the essential details of their bodies. There was a rich, black carpet that acted as a most suitable backdrop to naked flesh. Elegant period tables against the walls held a display of Griselda's tools of her trade as well as crystal glasses and decanters of wine. A gilded ceiling boss supported the pulley and rope of a fine, Victorian wall winch and in suitable places there were a few mahogany and leather items of furniture clearly designed for the positioning and, if necessary, restraint of a person.

Lucille felt her senses draining from her as she looked around and took in once again the familiar room, noting way the light from the many candles caused the mirrors to almost shimmer with a soft, warming luminescence that disguised the true purpose of the place. At such a time as this, Griselda said very little, when she spoke it would be to give simple, kindly but curt instructions. Lucille also knew from experience that there would be no taunting remarks when the woman actually used her, it was not Griselda's style. Rather when she spoke it would be to compliment or to encourage like guiding a horse over a difficult fence. It was carefully calculated, as Lucille well understood, for confrontational abuse would have been easy to resist, to fight against. The opposite, however, forced her to comply, to try and do better, to use her muscles to thrust our her sweet bottom to provoke and to tighten. To present her chest proudly, arms high behind her back or to acquiesce even to the ultimate terror of willingly opening her legs while she reclined upon the leather of the bench. How could she disappoint such caring words, how could she ever dare to fail, dare not to comply and fail to take far more than the screaming pain told her not to? On the few occasions that she had broken this trust, the tone of understanding rebuke had been mortifying and destroyed her, leaving her crying and far more desolate than the cruel use of any implement could ever had achieved.

Behind the mirrors she was conscious of the men's presence. She could feel them settling into the comfort of their elegant chairs, adjusting their clothes, lighting a cigarette, sipping from a long glass flute or opening their trouser fly a button at a time. But what she was most conscious of was the presence tonight of Griselda's candle. It stood grandly at the end of the room set in a polished wood, floor-mounted stick. It was white and long, like a phallus. It was not there to provide illumination.

Its slim length was clearly marked with black rings like some ancient time candle, and these rings did indeed provide the same service. Lucille had performed for it once before and so on this occasion was under no illusion as to how difficult this visit would be. The woman, Lucille's nemesis, was sitting comfortably watching her nervous little pet. Griselda was drinking and smoking a Black Russian set in the end of an equally black, long jet holder, the distinctive smell of Balkan tobacco added an exotic scent to the air of the room, mixing with her bespoke perfume. Her long, body-hugging evening dress was in imperial purple silk. She was obviously quite naked beneath it, as the sensuous details of her form could be clearly seen through the thin fabric. Her graceful legs were flattered by the fine fishnet of her stockings and the gleam of the black, patent, long healed shoes she wore.

Griselda at last removed the holder from her deep red lips and using it to gesture to Lucille, the light catching the thin gold band of the cigarette, she signalled that Lucille should undress. Lucille always had to wear the same clothes, white satin blouse, black pencil skirt, dark, fine stockings and court shoes. Beneath these she wore a perfect, white, expensive quarter cup brassiere and pure white, long-legged, silk knickers.

It would always start the same way, too, first disciplined across the tightened silk, then at some point Griselda's hands would carefully stretch and pull up the material so that it went deeply into the division between her round and smarting cheeks and the dripping lips of her sex, to now reveal the red lines that had already been left. Next the following strokes would fall upon her completely unprotected skin which would almost instantly reveal its fresh marks to the audience. Then finally, she would have to stand once again and slowly pull down the knickers and step out of them, this action, performed facing the hidden eyes, would cause her to know the humiliation of parting her thighs and exhibiting her shaven cleft for the first time. Lucille would then once more resume her position of submission and her punishment would begin, now cruelly and in earnest.

Carefully Lucille undid the blouse, a button at a time and finally slipped it off, to fold it and leave it upon a side table. She always watched her body constantly reflected in the vast mirror, as though observing another's disrobing in a dream.

Next she undid the neat row of buttons at the waist of the skirt and let it slide to the ground to then have to bend right over, bottom towards the one-way mirrors, to recover it. She stood there, watching the candle just as Griselda was undoubtedly doing; watching the jumping, yellow flame as it approached another ring. When the flame began to consume the ring in a cascade of melting wax, Griselda rose from her chair and with a nod signalled that it was time to begin. Lucille, with mounting terror, took up her place upon the purposeful, raised bench. She placed each of her stockinged knees into the padded divisions and bent her body forward over the brown, buttoned leather. In this extremely vulnerable pose she could see and, in time, intently watch the great candle; for there would be little pause in Griselda's efforts until the next ring was reached. In the still air of the room the candle always burnt very slowly.

Besides the reflection of her troubled face the wall mirror also permitted Lucille to watch each time the thin, long cane was raised and, of course, the moment of its decent.

As Griselda had once remarked, "The first, divine, anticipated taste of agony is always the sweetest to administer and observe." Her arm came down with all the energy it could muster and the first cry broke the stillness of the room. Through tear-filled eyes Lucille thought she could discern the candle flame flicker just a little, as the air was momentarily disturbed; but it was still such a terrifyingly long way from the next encircling line.

X   WATERY DREAM

W omen have never ceased to surprise me with the extremes
of their private erotic thoughts. When Michael Perkins
contacted me and asked me to write the most disturbing and
hard story I could think of for the short story collection he was assembling,
I drew upon a recurrent, masturbatory fantasy that a close female friend
of mine had kindly shared with me in some considerable detail. She may
well have been called Lucy or did she travel under another name? She
told me that time and time again she used it to bring herself to orgasm,
almost always achieving that at the same point of the story. Few, men or
women, will admit to going to such frightening places to seek arousal, but
many do. I have added a confusing twist at the end, one that she would
have liked to imagine. This tale is definitely not for the faint-hearted so
do skip it, if graphic and scary sadistic detail will offend…

T HE NIGHT WAS HOT AND THE THIN SHEET stuck to the sweat on
Lucy's body. Her fingers moved to her hard little button and
started to slowly rub. As her eyes closed and her mind drifted, she
was again walking along a crowded street. Then a car suddenly
drew up and she was wrenched from the pavement and removed
to a prison…

They all knew of this place, and there were some who had even
been there. At first she had sat upon the edge of the crude bed
in the small dark cell, with fear flooding her body. At nineteen
she was still very young and quite exceptionally attractive. Her
hair was almost a crop and her body was lean and hard from
constant sport, to the point of being muscular. Each of her young,

round breasts was capped with a dark areola that reared up like a miniature second breast; each had a long nipple, developed by the sucking mouths of countless boys since she was thirteen. She cropped her hair short between her legs, which suited her active life and the intensely hot, humid weather. The close stubble revealed her full mound with its neat tight slit below, two features of which she was justly proud. At the time of her arrest, she was wearing her smart work clothes, which now seemed out of place in these grim surroundings.

Other than water in the tap, she was given nothing. She used the crude hole in the floor to relieve herself. As the dim light of morning showed in the high, small window, the door opened to let two guards come in.

"Take down your knickers, pull up your skirt over your arse and lie face down on the bed. Don't cause trouble or we will hurt you." said one.

Frightened by his aggression, she quickly did as she had been told, revealing to them both the round fullness of her small attractive bottom. She lay on the rough blanket, facedown, feeling dreadfully exposed and vulnerable. Then hands pulled open the cheeks of her buttocks and she felt something cool being worked with a finger into her resisting sphincter. Hands still held her open and one of the men climbed onto her. She felt the hard end of what must be his prick forcing against her hole. It opened at the pressure and he slid right in, very big and very hard. Men had taken her there before, it was a method that she enjoyed even more than her cunt. She couldn't help feeling aroused. She resisted the sensation but she couldn't stop this natural stimulation happening. There was a momentary sharp pain as he went in as deeply as he could, this aroused her even more, and she cried out. Then he sodomised her with long, hard thrusts that made her gasp at each repeated entry.

She could feel him swell, pulse and come, it had been quick and she heard him grunt in satisfaction. Then the next guard was on her and inside her easily, as her anus was now expanded, open and lubricated, he went on longer. She hated it but it still aroused her beyond her control. She climaxed even before he did and the men both laughed. He then filled her with his orgasm. Without a word, though still laughing, they were gone.

What they had left in her slowly ran out as she eventually stood up. She felt a little sore and stretched. She waited until it had mostly left her body, then washed at the single tap. At last she felt she could dress again. She was sweating in the intense heat of the little cell. Somehow being used in this way, in prison, seemed different to her than if it had happened outside, in the normal world. It was as though she expected it to happen, that it was normal, par for the course. It made her angry, especially as she had to acquiesce and accept their instructions. Lucy was only too aware that this was but a taste of much worse to come. This prison had not achieved its whispered reputation for nothing. She had stupidly dabbled in fringe political matters, which was perhaps why she was here now. She knew that they tortured those they brought here, just as a matter of course, a routine for all inmates of either sex, but always worse for women. She had heard, in discussions with student friends, that they used electricity but beyond these vague rumours she knew very little. Such lack of knowledge, caused fear to mix with some strange, empty arousal; it gripped her to her very pit.

Later, much later, the door opened again and she was escorted from the cell and taken via endless, empty corridors to a room one floor below. There was no escaping the purpose of the dark, windowless room that smelt strangely of other people's fear. The unusual items that her eyes slowly took in were ominous in their presence. A man sat behind a cheap desk and she was motioned to sit in front of him.

"We are going to start you off by making you suffer a little." It was a simple blunt statement in a detached voice.

"You will of course want to reveal everything you know as things progress and certainly wish that you knew even more, just to try and make us happy. You are though small fry, worthless, stupid, full of the ideals of youth. What you tell us we already know, but you can try to impress us, try to please, try to stop your pain. I'm glad that you are both strong and young, you will stand up to things very well," he continued.

To Lucy, it felt as though he did this every day – which he did – and as though he was even a little bored with it all… which he wasn't… not with something as juicy as her. She was a little bonus to a job he already enjoyed, young, attractive and fit – such a pleasure.

"You are a very sexy little whore who will amuse my assistants, they work for the fun of it, as you will find out. I'm sure you won't disappoint. Just remember you have been very silly and this is your reward." He motioned with his hand. "Stand up and take off your skirt and pants. Remember always do exactly as you are told, it gets even worse if you choose to be difficult."

Lucy stood up and removed the items of clothing, placing them on the back of the chair. They looked with interest at the revelation of her expensive silk, French knickers. She stood there in her crisp white blouse, stockings, suspenders and smart heeled shoes.

"Off with the shoes!" he added.

His assistants then guided her to the wall, knowing already what had been planned for her. There was a drain in the floor beneath where she was positioned. They secured her wrists together quickly and hoisted them up by a rope to a ring. Then they pulled apart her ankles and fixed them to similar rings on the floor. She now straddled the grill of the drain, her delightful bottom fully displayed by the strain imposed by her posture and after they had tucked in her blouse. Rubber pipes, a bucket of water and a stirrup pump were produced.

"This is an old and most successful way of hurting a woman." he explained as she stared at the wall before her.

"It leaves no marks and applied with skill, causes no long-term ill effects. It can also be repeated again and again, as long as you have strength to endure. Think of it as a cross between a douche and an enema but far more extreme. It will be nice to see your womb distend and for you to feel your organs being squeezed. However, let us get on." He nodded to the men.

Throughout all of this, Lucy had said nothing. There had been no long preamble of interrogation; no reading of charges; no endless questions that she had prepared for in her mind. She had nothing to say, it was so very quick, so sudden, so terrifying.

Each pipe that ran from the pump was fitted with a special wooden end. One was thick and phallic, the other had a deep ring below its pointed head. Lucy had turned anxiously to see what was happening as the man had described things. She could see these 'things', these preparations, she could imagine where these pipes might go. Her blouse was now well tucked up into the strap of her bra. so that the lower part of her back was exposed and at the front in particular her abdomen. The special phallus was now worked with some difficulty into the closed line of her labia. She cried out as it forced its entry, stretching her inside and hurting, she cried louder when they pushed it through the opening of her cervix. Her buttocks were parted and the other pipe end pushed in, its deep ring to be gripped by the muscles of her sphincter. She could feel each device pressing against the other, her lower body completely engulfed.

They now, slowly and most carefully filled Lucy with long strokes of the pump handle. At first she could only feel the cold of the water rushing into her, finding what little room was left. As they continued, first came a wave of discomfort, then a growing sensation of real pain. It was a ghastly, rushing agony that was something like extreme menstrual cramps but much, much worse. Instinctively looking down, she could see that she was becoming swollen from the navel downwards. She tried not to cry out, to scream but they pumped with smaller strokes, adding water little by little. At each small increase she gasped and screamed as waves of gripping pain immersed her insides. Experienced hands tested her distension and when she was near fainting, they stopped. They knew their job well.

Now the man behind the desk got up and inspected the swollen womb for himself. His touch was gentle and she could feel his breath on the back of her neck. Lucy whimpered quietly, dreading another measure of water entering her.

"It hurts so much, young lady, doesn't it? he said at last, close to her ear, his fingers still played across the stretched skin even down to the distension of her mound. For a moment he paused and there was silence in the stifling room.

"Wake her up." He instructed. "Can't have you falling asleep and missing even a little pain." He said more intimately to Lucy.

One took up a short length of flat leather, which he wet methodically in the water bucket. Then he purposefully struck Lucy hard across one of the cheeks of her bottom as it pushed outward beneath her arched back. The shock more than the pain brought life back into her dimmed eyes and she cried out a different sound to the room. Another ten similar cuts had her wide awake and her hips and arse twisting and turning, deep red marks covering the tight flesh. This movement seemed to churn the water inside her and she screamed in a dreadful agony.

"Take out the pipes and let her drain." said the man.

They removed the nozzles. Almost instantly, water gushed from her and cascaded down the drain between her open legs. Lucy gasped large gulps of air at the sudden relief of the agony.

"We will fill you again in a while. This is not the last time your tough little body will stretch for us." said the man. "Turn her round and expose her tits." he instructed and returned to his desk.

When they had repositioned her to face out toward the room and stretched her even more so that her stockinged toes only just touched the ground and the rope at her wrists burnt. One carefully and slowly unbuttoned her blouse and opened it, then he produced a small knife from his pocket and cut the bra. at the middle, to free both breasts. Her large, hard breasts were stretched up to her armpits by her position, even so, they turned up at the end to point the nipples a little towards the ceiling. Her sex was framed quite beautifully by the white suspender belt, the labia now open from their recent penetration. The men stepped back to look at the fine, straining young body which was fully displayed and a wonderful sight.

The man behind the desk now spoke out, holding Lucy's staring eyes with his.

"Now, I want you to scream a little more for me, in between moments when you will inevitably pass out. We will continue for some hours. Don't worry, we will take our time and hurt you at your own pace. After all… you don't suffer when you have fainted." He turned to his men. "The hooks and the trolley…"

A cord was pulled down from a small pulley set in the old roof above her. At the same time, the other man pushed over a medical style trolley with apparatus upon it that was evidently electrical. One of them fixed two small steel hooks to the end of the pulley cord. Lucy screamed with fear as he approached. With deliberate force, he carefully thrust a hook through each of the full areolas, just behind the nipples, until the points of bright metal appeared again.

The pain was burning and instant; four moments of piercing pain for Lucy, causing sweat to run down her glistening, tanned body.

The man with the trolley, held up two long wires with small clips at each end. He looked enquiringly towards the man behind the desk?

"Her clit and her inner cunt lips, where she is wet." was the answer.

Instinctively, Lucy tightened the skin across her now flat abdomen, pulling back her hips in some futile attempt to back away from these clips. The man though, fixed them in place, carefully pulling back the little hood over Lucy's clitoris so the sharp teeth of the metal clip could bite into the erect purple bud. The teeth of the other clip were attached to an inner lip of the still gaping cunt.

"The flesh of the tits is stronger than you may think, we will now give them a new and more interesting shape." Explained the man to Lucy.

She watched, like a frightened bird, as a very heavy lead weight was fixed to the end of the cord. She watched in horror, pleading words of anticipation coming from her open mouth; as the weight was held aloft. At a nod from the man, it was let go. Lucy's body lunged forward as the heavy weight bottomed at the end of the slack and the hooks instantly pulled at the ends of her breasts without mercy.

Her beautiful rib cage, each rib defined, stood out, hollowed at her navel. Each fine breast now came to an exaggerated and extreme point, aimed at the ceiling pulley. The lead weight swung like a pendulum for a while as the room filled with a sad and dreadful scream. As the initial shock passed her cries turned to sobbing moans. Little drops of blood dripped from the tortured ends. Her feet were now completely free of the ground her body arched shuddering with spasms. They let this incremental pain soak through her, saturate her mind, as they contemplated her magnificent erotic display.

At each little movement of instruction from the man's hand. The control on the electrical machine was pressed and extraordinary but brief agony was transmitted to her most delicate places. These hideous bursts of pain where followed by involuntary quiverings of her lower body as it responded to the intensity of the waves of residual suffering. Eventually, Lucy lost control and urinated, sending her powerful spurt of yellow liquid onto the floor, to follow the water that had rushed from her womb, down the drain.

❋ ❋ ❋

Skilfully, Lucy had held back, savouring each new picture that filled her imagination in the dark of her room. It was the thought of peeing for this audience that at last overwhelmed her control. She tensed in a gripping orgasm that twisted and drove the muscles of her body and finally exited with the most sensitive of gasps from her mouth. She also really wet herself, warm liquid running between her parted thighs to mingle with the products of her sweaty, running cunt. Tomorrow her lover would be with her. She wanted him badly, in her arse, again and again. With this thought in her mind, Lucy fell into a deep sleep. Outside, the traffic hummed.

At the curb, a black car sat with its engine running, two men were at her door, they checked the address again on the arrest warrant by the light of a torch; one then raised his fist to start banging.

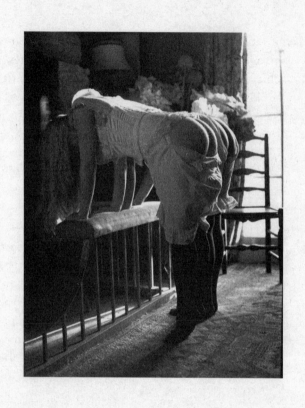

XI THE TWINS

THE STORY OF THE TWINS OF ST. LAWRENCE is important in the annals of the lives of women. Though they never achieved international fame a select few of the rich and influential of Parisian men spoke of them with awe.

They had grown up in the restricted and cloistered world of the late 19th century well-to-do. Christened Lucy and Monique and arriving half an hour apart, they had been born identical. Up to their early teens life had been pleasant enough, wanting for nothing and enjoying the love of a devoted mother. During their fourteenth year she died and, in his grief, their father became distant from them.

Feeling that they needed the help and guidance of a woman, he employed a highly educated but cruel and strict governess one Mademoiselle LaRoche. She was a pinched and bitter woman who had never found a man willing to take her on. She was soon most jealous and resentful of these two very attractive and lively girls and having convinced their detached father that their current standard of education was poor and their discipline even worse, she gained his tacit agreement to her being as strict as she felt necessary.

So their schooling became a daily hell. Mademoiselle Laroche would add up their failings, as she perceived them and at their bedtime treated their bare bottoms to the attentions of her thin Malacca cane. It was undoubtedly this regular punishment that welded them together. When they had received such treatment they would huddle together in the dark and console and comfort each other. Their bottoms would be soothed by the gentle rubbings of each other's hands and as their bodies developed, it was inevitable that they should find mutual pleasure in the caresses of their most intimate areas.

With youthful curiosity, swelling breasts were touched, first by the hand, the fingers teasing the nipples till they became swollen and hard, then by sucking with the lips and nibbling the erect ends. It was this action that led to the strange and powerful feelings that surged between their legs, the lips of their sexes opened and they became delightfully wet. Such cravings soon brought requests for the other's hand to be brought to bear beneath.

Step by exploratory step, and night by night, their naked bodies were investigated and understood. The work of expert fingers was soon replaced by a searching and teasing of quite agile tongues, for they would lie for hours with their heads between each other's legs, their orgasms were greeted with initial surprise, then greedily achieved. Some sixth sense would guide the movements of the tongue onto the hardened clitoris so that they would, with much practice come together, united in gasping spasms of raw pleasure.

Then at eighteen, as so often happened in those times, their father fell prey to an illness and in a short time died. Lucy and Monique were left quite wealthy but alone except for each other. Their dreaded governess was sent packing though they kept the little cane for they had found, as they grew older that their bottoms had become used to its effects to such an extent that it seemed to cause sensual stimulation in their intimate parts. They were therefore always at their most eager for satisfaction together after its painful use.

Until now, the twins had never mixed in Parisian society. Free at last to do what they wished, they moved to an apartment in the heart of the city and commenced to enjoy its delights to the very full. Always together they would attend the opera, plays and eat at fine restaurants. The twins were stunningly beautiful, their blond hair, that flashed and sparkled under the newly installed gas lamps, surrounded faces that radiated a perfection of youthful excitement. Lucy and Monique were tall and long-legged with corseted wasp waists which accentuated their high breasts. Beneath the sensual shimmer of their expensive silk dresses, the world could admire their almost boyish bottoms.

The city wanted desperately to know them, especially the men. One such beauty would have been novel enough, the two identical young ladies, seen together arm in arm, amazed and excited comment wherever they went. However, not surprisingly, they were unable to cope with the male of the species. Endlessly they discussed the subject of men and they had their maids obtain forbidden books and read of the activities that men and women practiced in private. Some of the stories carried illustrations and the erect male organ, exaggerated by the artists, together with its placement into the vagina, became the main talking point and fascination of the twins.

Of course their probing fingers had only been able to enter each other a modest amount, now they were mature, their small hands could though go further and stretch and probe their hidden places. These entries could not in the twins mind's match the penetration of the illustrated penises they saw pictured. So experimentally they tried the handles of various things like those of a whalebone hair brush. Though these trials felt quite different they were cold and lifeless and though new sensations were experienced, Lucy and Monique agreed together that they could not provide a substitute for the real thing. What they also agreed on was that they couldn't split up and seek a man alone, for they had for too long come to rely on each other for support. Everything, every new experience of life, had been arrived at together and so they wanted to come to the knowledge of men in exactly the same way.

Up to now they had refused, with shy, gentle smiles, the offers to dance, to join a table or to walk in the park, that had come from males of every shape and age. Each had thought he would succeed where all others had failed. Occasionally two men, out together, would make an approach, it was this possibility that seemed to hold the answer for Monique and Lucy. So it was resolved that the next suitable and attractive pair of men that approached them, would be 'tested' and if found agreeable, would be invited back to their apartments. Then it was hoped that their wishes to advance their sexual experience would reach fulfilment.

Their patience was soon rewarded. Two men, tall and suave in their evening dress, came over to the twins table at their favourite restaurant a few nights later.

Disappointingly, the men seemed to lack a certain confidence in their approach, for the twins' reputation made the manoeuvre but a token, playful try. The surprise, even shock, that signalled itself on those dark, lean faces, set above their impeccably starched winged collars, when the twins actually invited them to join them, made the girls squirm with ill concealed delight. Monique and Lucy were also somewhat relieved that saying yes to the tentative question had been so easy.

Introductions accomplished, more chairs were brought and champagne called for. Every man and woman in the establishment, waiters included, familiar as they were with the twins' reputation, stared in complete disbelief before entering into an earnest debate with their friends and partners. Gossip was indeed rife.

Though technically virgins, the twins conversed with the men like experienced and worldly women. The girls were well educated by book and little cane but beyond this they radiated a deep sexuality from their pale and far-from-innocent blue eyes. Sentences containing words which held a double meaning, were seized upon and enlarged, twisted about coyly but with an underlying confidence. The men were excited and encouraged by this and the diners around them picked up upon the extraordinary, buoyant mood of the table. When the evening ended the invitation to return to the twins' apartment was greeted with thinly disguised jubilation. The possibility that they were but being played with by the twins did not escape the mens' minds. It could well be that this notoriously unassailable pair of girls might be but teasing their eager pricks? What did it matter? they thought, for they had scored where all others had failed up until now. This would enhance their reputation, what ever transpired, and provide them with a story to tell at dinner for months to come.

The girl's apartment was tastefully comfortable. Their maids brought wine into the spacious sitting room and were then dismissed for the night. Conversation, aided by the alcohol continued, neither party quite knowing how to move on to more serious matters of the flesh. Lucy finally steered the conversation round to the subject of their youth and to the governess and her ways with the little cane. Barriers were slowly broken down. One of the men asked if he could see the implement of punishment when told that they had kept it. As it had attained a certain revered place in their lives, they had commissioned the making of a rosewood and silver mounted box for it to reside in and it was this long, polished box that was laid upon the table. With a certain ceremony one of the twins opened it. The exceptionally thin Malacca cane was about two and a half feet in length, it lay there rather innocently upon a bed of red velvet. At the sight of it the twins felt that pressing urge growing inside them. The men could see the flush of excitement in the girls' faces, with a look to his companion, one reached over and picked up the cane. First weighing it in his hand, he gripped it and swished it a few time sin the air.

Lucy stood up and with a tremor in her sweet voice, asked if they would like an explanation as to how their governess would use it?

"Perhaps I could play the part of the governess?" the man holding the cane asked.

"It was always like this." Lucy explained in answer and knelt down onto a footstool, bending her head low and gripping the legs of the stool. Lucy's' dress tightened across her bottom and Monique pointed out that the cheeks would always have to be bare, so with delicate movements she lifted her sister's skirt. Then her fingers unlaced the back-flap of the knickers. The return of the old ritual had temporarily made the twins forget the object of the evening's tryst, as the man raised the cane to bring it down upon the bared bottom which was already tensing in anticipation of the first stroke, Monique raised her hand and remarked that he had a stick of another kind with him that both she and her sister were very interested in seeing and not only his but that of his friend's. He immediately broke into a broad smile.

"Why, this is a game more to my taste." At this he quickly undid the buttons of his trousers. "Is this the stick to which you allude?"

Like a small serpent rising to strike, his penis appeared as large and as exciting as both girls could have hoped for. Without any further comment he quickly and before their eager eyes, undressed totally. This lithe, hairy man now proudly displayed what was better to the girls than a thousand naughty pictures.

Lucy made to rise from her position on the stool but the man stopped her and placing his hands on her hips pushed himself in-between her slightly parted legs so to enter her offered sex. It proved difficult at first to find the hole and Lucy frustratingly couldn't help as she needed both hands to support herself.

"I'm afraid that I need some help," he said to Monique. "Come and guide me into your sister."

Monique came forwards slowly, shy of touching this magical thing. The other man, sensing reluctance on her part came behind her and gently guided her hand, offering encouragement as he did so. Monique closed her fingers around the base of the organ, at the same time asking her sister to open her legs wider, which she did to the extent of the width of the stool. Then Monique pushed the swelling end into the wet opening she knew so well. The man felt the tip slip into the woman and asked Monique to relinquish her hold, which she still so firmly applied.

Monique watched as the man's buttocks rose and fell and took note of the whitening of her sisters knuckles and the sounds she was now making. As she continued to watch, quite transfixed by the display, she became aware of hands squeezing her breasts. Turning she found the other man now also undressed and with a toy bigger and more frightening than that of his friend. As he continued to fondle her he pushed it against her thigh so that she felt it hard and unyielding through her dress. Passion surging in her groin she continued to observe the copulation taking place before her but she, at the same time, aided and assisted the man's attempts to remove her dress.

Soon Monique was in but her corset, stockings and vest. She

had willingly slipped out her breasts as she like them to be played with and pulled down her drawers. Her man now laid Monique on her back across the chesterfield. With authority he forced up her legs until the thighs press against her bare breasts and her vulva was wonderfully displayed through its tangle of hair. Then he was upon her, keeping her folded and pushing into the girl with little difficulty. For Monique it was a moment of unique pleasure as she felt him slide in so deeply. It was even noticeably warm and of course filled both her vagina and her mind to bursting. When he started to push it in and out the feelings that emanated from deep inside her brought uncontrolled gasps and cries.

He gained momentum and with this her own passion rose further. He leant forward and gripped her under the bottom and his penis formed an arc inside her, its root rubbing her clitoris. He noted with satisfaction the effect this had on her. Monique at last came when this was being done to her, feeling an orgasm unlike any that she had experienced with her sister. Cries from the stool indicated that Lucy had also arrived. Seconds later a sensation that Monique was completely unequipped to deal with touched her cervix, a burning warmth hit it, coupled with the rhythmic expansion of his tool. She realised shortly afterwards that this must have been a man's release. To her it felt as the highest of all sensations, a subtle thing, to be savoured like the finest wine.

The men were ecstatic with their achievement, which went far beyond any possible expectations. The women were exhausted but equally happy that this new experience was all that they had dreamed and talked of it being. They sat around drinking, three now naked and one but with her drawers open. When they recovered their composure then laughing cries started up of 'shame' and 'undress' directed at sweet Lucy. She stood up and entertained them with a saucy, amateur strip that was slow and provocative. All now prepared by their nudity, the party adjourned to the bedroom. As they romped around on the great bed, holes wet and dry, back and front, red lips and pink lips, soft deep mouths and hard, hairy organs became confused. The worst thing was that the girls were identical nude as well as clothed. They played games with the men, changing names and teasing them. Finally, sleep, sex and wine overtook them and it was a startled maid who found this intertwined group in the light of morning.

Once tasted Monique and Lucy gorged themselves on the male root, always though from now on, being careful to request the men to discharge on their breasts or arses for fear of getting with child. Some time it was pairs of men as the first time, at others one between the two of them, especially if he was beautiful. Men were driven mad in these situations as the young, eager bodies devoured what they had to offer. Only one could have the prick at any time so an eager, empty crutch would be planted where his straining tongue could reach.

At times, when the fancy took them, out would come the little cane, the starting place of their desires. They would use it on each other as the men looked on leaving tantalising red lines on each other's perfect flesh. Occasionally a gentleman would be asked to oblige with his stronger arm, the twinned bottoms offered and bent over, side by side, wriggling for his pleasure. It was all 'great fun', as the girls put it. Society was a little shocked, even Paris society. It wasn't so much what was done, for after all that went on everywhere, it was more the ruthless way in which they consumed men. Never the same twice and the gentlemen waited eagerly for their turn to come. The twins played cruel games with some suitors, often rejecting one or more again and again until they became demoralised. For it was considered a must for a young man to achieve success with the twins. Only the best were picked however and many went unrewarded, almost excluded from the small elite that had.

Rumour circulated that they had dyed their pubic hair different colours, so that at last they were distinguishable, at least when their cunts could be admired. Men claimed that 'Rouge' or 'Noir' as they came to be called, were different in their tastes or approaches, that for instance, Noir had a tighter hole or that Rouge's breasts were definitely bigger. Opinions often became heated in Paris clubs as each defended the merits of the twin of his experience or his fancy. The twins heard of this and promptly changed colours regularly after that, though they didn't change their habits till, as age crept on, they retired gracefully from Paris society. Until the death of a generation, the red and the black were spoken of with fond memories, meaningless nicknames to those who had never rolled and loved for a night with those girls, each blessed with an identical gift to please others, albeit pleasing at the same time, themselves.

XII   THE WHIPPING POST

This account was found by accident in the diary of a young man working in the foreign service.

Of all symbols of torture and punishment there is none more powerful that the vertical finger of a whipping post. They have been, until recent times, almost always publicly displayed at the centre of a town, or in a prison yard. Even when they have been hidden within a dark chamber, they are still there in our minds. They come in every shape and form of complexity and decoration, yet their purpose is clear and unequivocal in function. Whether we are cruel rake or prim virgin, when an attractive young woman is affixed to such a post, our undivided interest is guaranteed.

We might enjoy, we might be aroused, we might shed a tear of sympathy but always we have had to watch, to be drawn deeply to the spectacle, for no stage has ever held its audience so tight or by such an evil thong as the union of the whipping post and those who taste the rare suffering of such a captivating victim.

"I had struck up a reasonable friendship with a Major in charge of the local garrison. Over cards one evening, he paused to ask me if I had ever seen a beautiful young woman whipped. I answered, with surprise at such a question, that I had not. He then explained that he had been asked by the Governor to instigate the punishment of the Governor's mistress who had in some way incurred this man's wrath. It was quite normal, it seemed, for women to be whipped within the town's fort, a service that he personally undertook for the local magistrate when both men and women were sentenced to such a punishment. This he felt would be a little different as the mistress in question was young, of fine beauty and some distinctive breeding and education.

I was so intrigued and curious by the offer and it would have seemed churlish to have declined, so I duly made myself known to the gate house of the fort on the appointed day and time. I was somewhat surprised to find that I was by no means the only audience. A double semi-circle of chairs had been laid out in the shade and most of these were taken by a gathering of those of importance in the area, both men and women. I paid my respects to a few with whom I already had some acquaintance and took my seat. A number of servants were running to and fro with chilled drinks, the entire event being something of a party.

Before us in the harsh sun was the central object of the occasion. Mounted upon a weathered and stained wooden dais was a most substantial, aged, wooden post. Large old iron rings were fixed in various places and it was capped with a dignified ball and spike finial. It was indeed a frightening device of official correction. Suddenly a hush fell and the small talk died away as into the area walked the Major, who nodded respectfully to the gathering. Behind him marched a number of his soldiers and between two of them walked a very attractive young woman, twenty years old, at the very most.

She was dressed in a demeaning, simple white cotton undergarment, yet she held her head erect and her softly darkened skin and dark hair showed well in the sun. Through her scanty covering, as she moved, I could already see a strong and long-legged body: her breasts forced out the cloth at her chest in a provocative way and I was immediately both aroused and captivated.

This vision did not seem to escape the young woman next to me who flapped her fan more vigorously and then turned to me with a hint of fire in her eyes to proclaim with ill-disguised enthusiasm that the victim was to be 'double sided'. At my obvious puzzlement she was happy to explain that the victim would receive the whip to both the front and rear of her body. Always, (she went on to enlarge) far more entertaining, especially when they were so 'fit', to use her word, and would therefore provide much 'sport'.

The young lady, flushing a little beneath her powder, added that, "The girl looks spoilt and sassy and certainly needs showing her place and taking down a peg. Nothing like a good brisking with the thong to teach them some respect and curb their willful ways."

Not knowing what to answer I nodded and she turned back to watch leaning forward upon her chair. While this woman had been clarifying my ignorance, preparations had been taking place. The soldiers had placed heavy leather restraints upon the girl's wrists and ankles and a muscular, dark soldier had appeared, stripped to the waist and wet with sweat. In his hand he held a whip which seemed to consist of three, thick, platted lashes each of slightly different lengths, the last eight inches or so of each, a single thong knotted many times.

The Major turned to address the audience and after welcoming us, explained in formal tones, that the punishment would consist of thirty six strokes to the back and the same to the front of the girl. The woman next to me now muttered in a knowing way under her breath, that sixty each side would be far more of a sensible dose for such an impudently proud young whore.

The Major now signalled to his men for the matter to proceed.

First a strong rope was passed through a ring at the top of the post and the end of this was tied to rings on the girl's wrist straps. Next, a wooden box was placed at the foot of the post and the girl made to climb up upon it. Then with swift progression, a burly soldier pulled with strength upon the rope, which drew the hands above her head and forced her to rise on tip toe. Her back was towards us and as most of her shoulders were bare one could see the shoulder blades closed tightly together and the muscles straining with this action. Ropes were now quickly affixed to the ankle cuffs and as the box was pulled out from beneath her toes, the ankles were pulled out by the ropes to rings set in the platform to either side, drawing her legs apart some four feet or more. Hanging like this, with the full weight of her body on her wrists, the pain experienced inevitably drew a gasping cry from her lips. Her back seemed even more magnificently stretched and her buttocks filled out the thin cloth delightfully.

At a nod from the Major, a soldier reached up to the cotton shift and grabbing it with his hand at the top, proceeded to rip it methodically down her body. Only when the garment hung in tatters, held only between her body and the post, exposing the entirety of her back and bottom, did he withdraw. The dramatic stripping of this woman drew a further gasp from the group, especially from the ladies. Her body was indeed most beautiful, stretched, as it was, by her taxing suspension; the muscles were exceptionally tight and strained down her back to her bottom which consisted of two strong, full and very rounded haunches, with a deep, clearly defined division between. These capped her long thighs, which were well shaped and almost athletic. I noted with some personal embarrassment that it was quite possible to see the generous form of the distended lips of her sex at the apex. At this sight I felt myself – and my organ – stir most uncomfortably.

The large man with the whip now approached and as I watched I could see fresh beads of sweat forming on the rich colour of the sun-kissed back bared before him. He swung the three feet or so of leather loosely in his hand and seemed to be contemplating the task before him. After re-positioning himself a few times and planting his feet to make a stable platform, he reached back his arm to deliver the first stroke with practiced ease. The movement when it came was slow and yet deliberate, for there was weight in the instrument. It landed with a sharp crack upon the virgin flesh drawing a triple line from the side of her round breast to fully across the centre of her back. Tightened though she was, her body still managed to twist with the obvious pain but little sound came from her.

One after the other, the strokes fell, always though with a long and precise pause between. Each blow was laid to a different place, the back, the cheeks of her bottom and the top areas of the thighs in rotation and here at the thighs the thongs wrapped well round each leg to draw a special straining and writhing from the girl's body that ended in dramatic shudders. It was also these particular strokes on such a sensitive area that brought from her at last her first real cries.

The Major, as each cut was given, pronounced the number in a curt and formal tone but at each successive crack of leather on skin, the cries lasted longer and eventually almost drowned him out to our ears, each great scream now tailing away into a gasping sob. The man with the whip now worked differently, placing instead his strokes upon the areas where he had already left his angry triple wheals. This had the effect of drawing blood as these wheals now burst open in response to the additional, deliberate cuts. I was mesmerized but had I thought that this display was breath-taking, it was to be nothing to what was to follow for both erotic drama and obvious cruelty.

At the reaching of the allotted thirty-six strokes, the trembling, moaning woman was turned. This was done by simply releasing her ankles and rotating her bodily upon her suspended wrists.

When the ankles had been secured again, though this time pulled even further apart till her legs were straining at her hips, the last few scraps of cloth were ripped from her and she was displayed fully naked.

Though her beautiful, youthful face was gripped in agony it was still alive and proud, her body from the revelation of this view, was even more wonderful. Dark hair fell from her head to cover her shoulders and the rivers of sweat that now washed her made her gleam like polished bronze in the sun. Her breasts were large, full and hard as a reflection of her youth, their line ran seamlessly into the deep hollows of her distended, straining armpits where dark, moist curls lay. The end of each breast was capped with a long hard nipple and a large, dark, swollen areola.

The sides of each breast bled a little, where the tips of the lashes had found this so tender flesh. Beneath the display of her ripe chest, the lean stomach was deeply hollowed, centred by a shadowy navel and showed the full shape of the rib cage. Tortured, stretched, abdominal muscles stood out as ridges and the curve of her belly was drawn tight like a drum skin. Her extremely prominent mons was hairless, as is the custom in this part of the world, and the polished, plucked mound quite gleamed as it rose with pride above the incision of her sex. The excessive and difficult parting of her legs completely exposed her mature vulva for all to see and the engorged sweet lips were wet with her involuntary juices and well parted, clearly showing the inner folds.

I took in this unique sight even as a bucket of water was thrown over her head, no doubt to revive her senses to every touch of pain that was yet to come. The water ran red upon the boards beneath her as it washed the wounds at her rear. At this she seemed to come alive and cursed and swore at the men before her with a language and aggression that belied her tender years and quite took me aback.

This coarse outburst made the Major turn to his audience with a smile of satisfaction, as though he had almost hoped for the excuse to state that such ill manners must be cured. They had just the subtle methods for those who had not yet learnt to be submissively respectful during punishment.

"We shall 'divide' her," he stated to the audience, "which will concentrate her mind, I feel sure, and teach her better ways." The Major paused for a breath. "And," here again her played to his eager crowd, "as she is so well suited, the 'nooses' as well, I think."

At a nod from the Major the man with the lash seemed to know what was meant by these suggestions. He tucked the wooden handle of the whip under his arm and using both hands deliberately using his finger tips, forcefully opened her labia so that the inner lips gleamed like jewels and her clitoris showed now its purple head at the junction. Then to a round of delighted applause from the audience, especially my female neighbor, he forced the whip handle with its large round pommel, deep into this engorged place, working this wooden rod around and in and out to further stimulate and open her sex. She moaned and shook at this forced entry with the result of this attention leaving her stretched sex fully open as her legs were so painfully parted.

This I assumed to have been the 'dividing'; the nooses were

more obvious. A solider produced two circles of leather thong from the base of the post and using the box to stand upon, he deftly placed first one then the other around the base of the girls breasts. They were each a leather noose and he pulled upon the thongs till they tightened and bit deeply into the flesh so that she winced. Now each breast was as a round ball darkening and hardening like ripe fruit, engorged by its restricted blood flow. The thongs were tied off behind the post so also pulling these orbs provocatively apart.

"I'm so glad she has had the nooses." confided my helpful companion, turning to me. "Such a young bosom can only benefit by being hardened so, she will learn from a different pain there now when the lash gives them its bruising kiss. I often have it done to my maid when she displease me, it is so educational especially if a crop is used."

If I had met this lady next to me under other circumstances I would have expected her to have discussed the changes in her garden or to have shown me her poems. I had never before considered the sadistic qualities of the women of her class, and therefore the sexual fire in her eyes was a great shock to my relative innocence.

Satisfied by these detailed improvements, he took up the whip and changed his position. His next stroke was delivered very skillfully using an upward twist of his wrist, causing the thongs to land with full force between the girl's legs. I could clearly see the flashing knotted tips of the leather lashes drive viciously deep between the open lips, even partially within her gaping entrance. The scream that came was a new sound, as though a supreme pain, as yet undiscovered, had been tasted. The body thrashed and tore at its bindings which, sadly for her, failed to yield. It was now crystal clear to me, just as to how the Major intended to gain her respect for her punishment.

Even before the naked body had settled from its convulsions a similar stroke was again laid to this sweet place of pleasure and love, with frightening and deliberate cruelty. Again came that animal scream that now hardened my own member as never before.

The woman beside me was uncontrollably clapping her hands with sadistic glee, other women seemed clearly flushed with sexual emotion, even rocking slightly in their seats, at this rare and harsh torture.

It took the man six of his last thirty six strokes each applied to the ripe sex and mound to break his victim. Blood from her whipped place ran down the inside of each of her thighs and dripped upon the ground. At the last strokes to this place her screams dwindled to be replaced with child-like cries and pleading whimpers. Her body now trembled and shuddered in uncontrollable muscle spasms that made her even more sexually beautiful, seemingly in a massive orgasm, which perhaps it was.

They paused to bring back her senses with another bucket of cold water thrown hard into her face yet even after that, her head hung down and her eyes were dark, glazed pits. Though they had wanted her broken, the lash had not finished in its harsh work and her armpits and abdomen were flogged till they bled. The man saved the last dozen strokes for her bound breasts, these an area of great tenderness for any woman and now such tenderness enhanced by the cut of the thong around them. He worked skillfully between first one and then the other seeing that their soft, undersides and swollen pointed ends were equally bruised and crushed by the cutting whip till each was a bloody orb. He must have been well satisfied with the results of his knowledge and expertise, for this final action found for her another new and terrible pain and so revived her long silenced cries. It also promoted her to loose control of her bladder and drench the blood stained boards below with long pulses of her urine.

When they took her down she was a broken trembling form. I think she was unconscious or near to that state for as they carried her out, for she made no sound that I could hear.

Now I was, with some shame, addicted to this punishment of a woman and returned many times to see young female criminals flogged, occasionally even between their opened legs. I became hardened to the extremes of cruelty that were quite normally sanctioned by the local courts for fairly petty offenses, though none would ever better this first moment and the exceptional body I had seen suffer so exquisitely and with such wondrous pride, its glorious battle with the leather lash burned upon my mind for ever.